Not Perfect

Gaya Hawke

Contents

①

My stomach churns, bile rising before I can even think twice about what's happening. I rush to the bathroom, pushing my door open roughly. It's barely past seven so my stomach is still empty. Not that I even have an appetite when I'm feeling like this.

I try to recall what I had for dinner yesterday. The Miller's dinner party is all that comes to mind. It must be food poisoning or simply from the shrimp they served.

I feel nauseous, the hair sticking to my forehead due to my damp skin. I decide to take a shower, getting a change of clothes from my room. I turn on the water and remove my clothes.

The coolness of the water makes me feel better instantly. I step out after lathering vanilla scented body wash on.

My mind keeps thinking back to a few weeks ago. I find myself panicking, knowing it could be possible. The dates add up, and I know I've read somewhere that some people don't show for a while.

I swallow the lump in my throat, grabbing my keys and purse. My parents would question why I'm leaving so early, pretending as if they care about my wellbeing.

As predicted the two of them sit at the dining room table. The smell of food makes my stomach grumble, and not of hunger. I try to keep it down, taking slow breaths.

My dad notices me first, setting his coffee mug down. "Where are you heading to so early?"

I step closer to the table, avoiding my mothers stare. "Alice and I agreed to have breakfast together."

He nods, going back to reading on his cellphone. My mother clears her throat, a brow arched.

"Your sister is coming tonight, don't make any plans." The way her eyes dare me to argue makes me feel defeated.

She's well aware that my older sister and I have the rockiest relationship on earth. It began as soon as I was born, Holly absolutely hated me. I guess she was spoiled and used to being the center of attention.

Now we're older, and she's never tried to mend things. It doesn't help that my parents adore her, and look at me as if I'm not their own creation.

Finally escaping the house, I climb in my car. I remember why I'm going to the store and sigh. If it's positive, I'll have to tell my ex-boyfriend. After the two of us shared a night I always thought of as special, he ended things. My father owns part of a business in town, Thomas always dreaming of working there.

After the two of us graduated last year, he worked his hardest to convince my dad that he was qualified. I helped at my dads' office since I took a year off despite how upset it made my parents. I overheard Thomas telling one of the guys there.

His parents are equally wealthy, but his interest was doing business, not fashion, or editing magazines. Now I'll feel even worse if I am carrying his child. I still have options, but because I'm stubborn, I always go with what I think is best. My parents don't have a say in this, not when I've devoted my entire life to trying to make them proud.

I pull into the nearest drugstore and park my car, sitting there for a couple of minutes before finally getting the courage to go inside. The summer heat immediately hits me, making me wish I wore less clothing. The automatic doors open, cool air hitting me as I walk in.

I walk to the aisle that holds various different types of tests. It's overwhelming and I find myself getting three different brands.

And because I haven't had breakfast, I grab a bag of sour patch kids.

Placing the items on the counter, I smile at the older woman.

Her golden brown hair has hints of gray. "Hi honey, will that be all for you?" She asks after ringing them up.

I nod, swiping my card. The price of the three tests combined is insane. I take the bag, wishing her a good day. As soon as I start my car, the ac turns on. I sit for a couple of minutes, enjoying my candy.

I contemplate going to Thomas house and taking them with him there. I even consider calling my friend, knowing she'll be supportive. But for some reason, I want to do this alone.

I want to have time to prepare, and having anyone around might make me feel ashamed. I'm used to dealing with things on my own.

When I arrive, I'm relieved to see my parents' main car, not in the driveway. Stepping out with the bag in my hand, I nervously unlock the front door. I kick my shoes off at the front, closing the door behind me.

I make sure to grab a bottled water from the kitchen to calm my nerves. I lock the bathroom door, opening the three boxes and taking the digital one first.

I'll take one first, and try again later. I repeat to myself that I'll be okay. No matter the results, I can handle it. But even that doesn't help the fact that I could be carrying a baby.

I read the back of the box, doing as it says. Waiting the suggested time, I mindlessly scroll through my phone. Too distracted to even pay attention to anything. When the timer on my phone rings, I almost jump off the counter.

My nerves are doubled as I stare at the stick that's faced down.

Breathing in and out I bite my lip. "I can do this," I mutter with a shaky voice and hands.

Counting down from five, I flip the stick over, practically holding my future in my hands.

I frown, seeing it still loading. My brows crease until a word pops up. I feel myself freeze, my heart hammering against my rib cage.

Pregnant.

(2)

After the shock had subsided, all I felt was determined. I was aware of my options, and that I didn't have to put myself through this. But the reality of this situation is that I want to. Even if my parents kick me out, which I'll leave either way. I have the money to raise a child. No one has to tell me that it'll be difficult, I know it will be.

A kid isn't a pet, they're around forever and my choices will affect their lives. The only bright side to my situation is that I'm fortunate to have money saved up. I can easily get a job, move into an apartment, and keep saving up. With that in mind, I feel ready to tell Thomas and then my parents.

After I took the first pregnancy test and my heart dropped, I took the second one two hours later. It was almost like I was hoping for it to be true. Yet part of me wanted it to be false. I spent the rest of the afternoon locked in my room. I researched and read through blog posts. Wanting to know as much as possible.

My sister came over for dinner, luckily she brought her boyfriend so she left me alone. I was excluded from every conversation which didn't bother me at all for once. I fell asleep right after, allowing the four of them to catch up.

This morning I was full of determination. Ready to just get the mess out of the way and deal with things slowly.

I text Thomas, asking if he's home. He responds right away, asking what I want. It's been three weeks, and I've seen him a handful of times. He doesn't try to talk to me anymore, but he never fails to give me a small smile. One that is his way of apologizing without words.

I tell him that we have to talk before changing into a pair of jean shorts and a gray tank top. The temperatures have gone insanely high, making me sweat at the mere thought of stepping foot outside.

I put my hair up before slipping on my shoes. Walking downstairs, I can hear the television on a news channel playing.

My father sits in his office, having a cup of coffee before he leaves for work. I'm surprised to see my sister here so early but she often drops by before work.

"I'm going out," I call out, making it to the door before my mom calls my name.

Moms heels sound throughout the kitchen. "You're not gonna greet your sister?" She asks.

To avoid a dispute, I keep my comment to myself. "Morning Holly."

Holly has always been the star child. The one with the perfect grades, social skills, and looks. Her hair is the exact same shade as my mothers, minus the hint of gray. She's almost identical to her.

Holly smiles, her eyes showing anything but kindness. "Thomas doesn't come around anymore? Oh, wait, he was using you." She pouts in mock concern.

I clench my teeth together, willing myself to keep it in. "I'll be back later," I mutter, walking away.

I calm myself before driving to the house I once spent all of my time at. The three-story home looks exactly like every house in the neighborhood. It's perfect cream paint color and white fencing being the only difference.

Taking a deep breath, I get the positive pregnancy test that I wrapped in a napkin. Putting it in my back pocket, I walk to the front door.

I wait while the doorbell rings, repeating in my head that it'll be fine. Thomas isn't a bad guy, he was very sweet until I overheard how he was using me. He promised that he truly loved me but his plan was that at the beginning.

Either way, I wouldn't allow anyone to use me and lie about it for over a year.

The door opens revealing Thomas, his lips turn up slightly.

"Hey." He replies after staring at me for a few seconds.

I wipe my sweaty palms discretely on my shorts. "Hey, can I come in?"

He nods, opening the door a bit wider. "Of course."

He leads me to the kitchen. "Want anything to drink? We have sweet tea." He adds.

It was my favorite when I came over. I nod, looking around the perfectly decorated kitchen.

Pouring us both a glass, he hands me one. "Should we go to my room?" He asks.

"Sure." I set the glass down after drinking half of it.

We walk up the stairs, the several pictures of them lined on the walls. Their mother loves to have their home represent them as a family. They love traveling and visiting new places as a family.

Something I've always been envious of. But the few times they invited me, I felt welcomed.Entering his bedroom for the first time in weeks feels nostalgic.

His bed is made, the dark gray sheets neatly folded. His collection of CDs are organized neatly and I remember the number of times he'd allow me to choose what to listen to.

I smile at the memories, meeting his gaze.

"Are you okay?" He wonders, crossing his arms.

I take the stick from my back pocket, deciding to just go for it. Dragging it on just makes me even more nervous.

I can tell he's confused, brows creased as he takes it cautiously. I feel the breath knocked out of me when he catches on. The way his mouth gapes open and his eyes widen.

Thomas runs a hand through his hair, tugging at the ends. "Shit, Bea." He mutters.

I bite my lip anxious at what he'll say. "Congrats?" I try to joke, my voice shaky along with my hands.

He breathes out a laugh in shock. "We're having a baby?" He asks in disbelief.

I nod to the proof in his hands causing him to look at it again. "Are you okay?" I ask, noticing how pale he looks.

With a nod, he hands it back to me. "I'm in shock, what have you decided?" Thomas sits beside me, the bed dipping a little.

I smile softly, fidgeting with the soft bed sheets. "To keep it." I watch his reaction. "What do you think we should do?"

Leaning forward he sighs. "I'll support you in anything. Your parents are gonna kill us." He mumbles the last part making me laugh.

I nod because his parents will probably accept it a little easier than mine will.

Thomas and I look at each other for a few moments before he breathes out a laugh. "We're actually having a baby.."

(3)

Anytime that Thomas or Alice asked me if I'd told my parents, I would change the subject. I knew I needed to tell them soon. Pushing it off was just easier than dealing with the scene it will surely cause.

Unexpectedly they were waiting for me to come down this morning. The tone my mother used was like every other time she's been angry. She doesn't leave room for argument.

They both wait in the family room, the air thick with tension. I sit on the chair across from them. Waiting for them to tell me what I did wrong. Assuming that it had something to do with work or school.

Dad holds a white sheet of paper out for me to take. It's a list, one side having items and the other dates, prices, and even times. My eyes immediately roam to the red pen that has been used to circle one of my recent purchases.

I completely forgot about it. It never crossed my mind to use cash to prevent my parents from finding out. I've always thought things through but my minds been a disaster. It's been nearly impossible to even remember what I'm doing.

I lift my head up to face them. This is it, I can see it in my mothers' eyes and the way my fathers' jaw ticks.

My mother crosses her arms. "Tell me this is a mistake?" Her voice is low and intimidating although I've heard it a million times.

I toss the paper on the coffee table, with my head raised I say, "I was planning on telling you."

Now it's dads turn to hold my gaze. "Tell us what? That you ruined your entire life?"

My father has always been a calm person. He hides his anger easily, better than my mom does. Growing up, he never raised his voice or punished us. He wouldn't give us that look to warn us as my mother did. He simply isolated himself and talked to us when he was calm.

I definitely took after him meanwhile Holly after my mother.

I swallow the lump in my throat, my mouth feeling unusually dry. "I'm having the baby," I say. "I'll figure things out afterward."

As expected my mother doesn't hesitate to try to control me. "Raising a child isn't easy. I will make an appointment and you will terminate this pregnancy." Her words would normally affect me. I'd allow her to control my life and let her walk away with the final say.

This time it's different. We aren't discussing something that can simply be undone, not without me standing up for myself. Before she can leave the room, I raise my voice for her to hear me loud and clear. I watch her turn back to me, raising a brow. With my eyes trained on hers, I repeat myself.

"I'm not doing that mom, I'm keeping the baby."

My dad rubs his temples in frustration. "Bea, your mother is trying to help you." He sighs.

I shake my head instead, allowing myself to say what I've always wanted to say. "She's afraid of the humiliation from the public. You're so used to having a perfect daughter and family image, that you're desperate to keep it that way. Too bad I'm not like Holly!"

Her usual green eyes are a darker shade, hiding any light in them. "You are nothing like Holly. We always wanted two perfect daughters to follow in our success. But here you are, ruining your life and disrespecting the two people who raised you."

I clench my teeth, feeling myself shake with anger.

"The day that I was born was the day that you three plotted to make my life a living hell. It's always been about Holly, I'm sick of it! I'm nothing like her and you should be proud, I'll never be as desperate for attention as she is!"

My mother's hand collides with my cheek, the sound of the slap echoing throughout the room. I hold the side of my face, feeling it throb as my vision becomes blurry with tears.

This is the second time that she has put her hands on me. And the second time that my own dad has watched with a blank stare. They both show no sympathy towards me.

Without another word, I rush upstairs. Once I'm calm enough I send Alice a message to let her know if went bad. She immediately responded and told me to drive to her apartment.

I pack some of my clothes and anything I can fit into the duffle bag and suitcase. Alice lives almost an hour away which will only help clear my mind. I'll also probably stop to get something to eat.

My stomach grumbles in hunger although the thought of food right now isn't helping. Looking around my room I make my bed and make sure I have what I need.

Taking one last glance before shutting the door and hauling the bags down the stairs. I can hear their low voices in the kitchen. It's difficult to sneak out quietly when I'm carrying two bags that ate my weight combined.

The chair scrapes when I've gotten my shoes on. I hear heavy footsteps behind me before my dad calls my name.

Dropping my hand from the doorknob I turn around. "Yes?"

He eyes the bags on the floor, raising a brow. "You're leaving?"

I nod, even if it's obvious enough. "I have to," I say.

"If you do as your mother says, you can stay." They don't seem to understand that.

"I know." I grip the doorknob, getting my bags on the porch. "Bye," I mumble, struggling to carry my things.

I don't look back, only hearing the door shut behind me. My main concern is fitting everything in my car. After some lifting and huffing, I manage to fit it all in my back seat.

The drive isn't bad since I stopped halfway for some food. Taking the time to let Thomas know where I'll be staying for the next three months or so.

Alice had a spare bedroom in her apartment that she had recently turned into the guest bedroom. As soon as I told her that I was pregnant, she completely made this room for me. It's true that she's been wanting us to be roommates since she moved away last year.

I've never been more grateful to have her in my life than I am right now.

(4)

For the past two days, I've been adjusting to my new room. Alice did great with decorating it. I've unpacked my clothes and other stuff I brought along.

I'm an expert at pushing my feelings aside and dealing with things a day at a time. Which is exactly what I have been doing. I haven't heard from my parents or even my sister. Thomas works with for my dad four times a week and mentioned him being stricter on him.

He always liked that Thomas was interested in business. I'm sure his opinion on him has changed by now.

I made an appointment here when I arrived two days ago. It was Alices' idea to get everything set up and to confirm my pregnancy.

Thomas was even set on attending every appointment with me. Despite the drive and the fact that he works today, he still drove to join me.

His yellow Camero pulls up beside mine. I grab my bag and meet him at the entrance.

"Good morning." Thomas smiles, holding the door open for me.

It's still weird for us to be talking. After our breakup, I promised myself that I would never say a word to him again. The irony, I'd have to see him for the rest of our lives now.

I sign my name at the front desk and join Thomas. His leg bounces when he's nervous and it doesn't help that it makes me feel worse.

I place a hand on this knee, he smiles sheepishly. "Sorry." He says quietly.

"Nervous?"

He denies it as expected. "Are you?"

My name is called and his question is answered when I nod. We follow the lady who gives us a kind smile. I let Thomas talk while I keep my mouth clamped shut.

We sit down and wait for the nurse to come in. It takes less than five minutes before she introduces herself and tells us what we'll be doing today. I almost feel embarrassed when she asks about my last period. I never kept up with it because of how irregular it was.

I had no other symptoms other than the recent throwing up. She assured me that it was fine and that most women go through that as well.

I'm around six weeks pregnant which sounds about right. We scheduled another appointment for our first ultrasound next week.

I had a urine pregnancy test done and I'm one hundred percent pregnant. Thomas asked questions and didn't seem to be nervous anymore.

Thomas walks me to my car, reading through the pamphlets we were given.

He finally looks at me. "How are you feeling?" He asks.

I shrug, "I'm okay. You?"

The heat becomes unbearable but I ignore it.

"I'm fine." He smiles. "Have you considered us moving in together?"

I avoid his eyes because he asked over the phone and I told him I'd talk about it later. My answer is no, I just don't know how to tell him that.

"It's not a good idea." I watch his expression.

Thomas sighs, stuffing his hands in his pockets. "I make enough money to rent an apartment for the three of us. You don't have to worry about any of it."

If we were still together, I'd say yes in a heartbeat. We always talked about moving in together and having takeout once a month. Things are different now and I know that moving together won't be easy.

"I'm staying with Alice for now."

He nods instead of arguing. I unlock my car, giving him a small smile. "You better get going before my dad does something crazy."

His lips turn at the corner. "You're right. Do you want breakfast first?" He asks.

I follow him to a restaurant down the street. Thomas only had twenty minutes so we wasted no time until he had to drive back. My dad is all about being professional, I can't imagine how he'll deal with Thomas being late.

He did tell him in advance but I doubt that will do much.

I drive back to the apartment and spend the rest of the time watching videos. I've been trying to prepare for what's to come in this pregnancy. I never took the time to think about how difficult it really is.

I'm in the easy stages according to everyone on youtube. I thought nausea and lack of appetite were bad only to find out that it gets much worse. I have a lot of preparing to do before any of that happens.

What really made me push my laptop far away from me was finding out about the actual birth. I decide that I've had enough of that and instead start on making lunch.

Alice should be home in two hours. I just watch whatever I can find on the TV and wait around for her. It gives me the motivation to find a job because I can't see myself doing this every day.

$$(5)$$

I t's Saturday meaning that Alice doesn't work today. I've been feeling cooped up and sick at the same time. The morning sickness makes me want to stay inside all day. But then I also feel like I need some fresh air.

Which is perfect because Alice wants me to meet her friends today.

We'll be meeting them at the mall in an hour. I joined her for coffee as soon as I had gotten out of the shower.

"Have your parents tried calling you?" She asks.

I purse my lips before replying. "No, I don't expect them to either."

She nods drinking her coffee. Her eyes light up as if remembering something. "My mom says congrats."

The mention of her makes me smile. "Have they left for their trip yet?" I wonder.

Alices' parents both love to travel. They don't have any responsibilities since Alice is old enough. There isn't a place they haven't visited.

"They leave next week. I wish I could go." She pouts.

I smile, "One day you'll be able to travel too." She could do it now but she doesn't want to do it alone.

Her smile widens as she fantasizes about visiting Hawaii. I empty what's left of my coffee and wash the cup.

"We should get ready, " I tell her, going to my room.

We'll most likely be walking around so I choose something comfortable. I've always been kind of serious, being raised by people who were so uptight all of the time. Making friends was fairly easy yet I find myself being nervous to meet her friends.

Alice described them all to me as easy going and down to earth. So I hope they don't hate me at first glance.

When we get to the mall, we walk towards the giant waterfall. I can tell it's them when we get closer and they all stand up. I have four sets of eyes on me as I give them a coy smile.

Alice stands beside me. "This is my friend Beatrice but she likes Bea better." She tells them. "Bea this is Chase, Chelsea, Jesse, and Matthew who hates being called that." She grins at his glare.

"Hey." I smile.

To remember their names I repeat them in my head. Chelsea and Chase are twins, light brown hair and green eyes. That's the only similarity they share and otherwise, you can only tell that they are even related.

Jesse has curly dirty blonde hair and blue eyes. If he's not the definition of a surfer than I don't know what is.

Matthew or Matt has dark hair and brown eyes. I would never approach him on my own. His inked skin and obvious muscles are enough to intimidate me.

We walk around the mall, Chelsea showing me the best stores. I buy a few things since I could only bring so much from my parents' house. It feels natural being around them.

It's just Alice and Chelsea beside me since the other three were hungry. They tried a couple of times to get out of it but Chelsea wasn't having it. She finally sighed and told them to go.

I sit with my phone while they continue to try clothes on. There's nothing I hate more than trying clothes on. I just wing I and get whatever looks like will fit.

Alice pokes her head out, looking for me. "You can go to the food court if you want." She smiles. "I know you'd rather be there than here."

"Are you almost done?" I stand up, more than happy to go.

She gives me a look before shaking her head. I laugh and tell her to join us when they're done.

The smell of unhealthy sweets and foods fill the air. I make my way towards the three that are happy to be away from the shopping.

"Hey, " I say, sitting beside Matt.

They wave or say something incoherent, stuffing their faces.

Chase stands up, wiping his hands on a napkin. "Do you like pizza?" He asks. When I nod he goes to the line.

I then plan to take him my money so he can pay but Matt tells me to sit. "He's got it."

Deciding not to argue I stay in my seat.

Jesse leans forward, acting as if he's interrogating me. "How old are you?" He asks.

"Nineteen, " I answer.

He nods, tapping his fingers on the table. "Okay, how did you meet Ali?" Never heard that one before.

I smile. "We met in middle school. we shared a class together." We became inseparable ever since.

His questioning is stopped when Chase comes back. He sets my pizza down along with a lemonade. I thank him, really wanting to pay him back.

He looks at Jesse. "Are you interviewing her?" He chuckles.

Matt tells me that Jesse is always like that and that I'll get used to him. I like that he has a sense of humor.

It takes twenty minutes for Alice and Chelsea to join us. They carry four bags each and we move to a bigger booth. I've gotten to know them each a little bit, learning about how they all met and such.

It was fun to be able to enjoy my first weekend here.

(6)

I made plans to start looking for a job today. I at least want to begin my search rather than sit around doing nothing. I've always been restless, I like working and being occupied. It gives my mind a break from over-thinking.

According to the internet, there are three shops at the beach that are hiring. The drive is less than twenty minutes away and I'm okay with that. Alice tried to convince me to not worry about any of the rent or bills. But if I'm staying with her I refuse to do it for free.

She's been extremely kind in letting me stay with her, I wouldn't take advantage of that. Which is why I'm currently here, determined to find a part-time job.

The beach isn't as crowded as I expected it to be. I did come before it supposedly gets packed.

As I walk to the shopping area I hear my name being called. I recognize their voice but have trouble finding where it's coming from. Stopping near the restrooms I turn around at the sound of shoes hitting the pavement.

I smile when I see Chelsea running towards me, she leans over to catch her breath. Jesse cackles behind her which causes her to roll her eyes.

"Hey," I say, stepping aside to let someone walk by.

She grins, tucking her hair behind her ear. "Hey Bea, how's life?" She acts casual, still out of breath.

Jesse stands beside us, wrapping an arm around Chelsea's shoulder. I can't tell if they're a thing or not. From what I've seen, the two of them are just close friends.

"Good, I'm looking for a job," I tell them.

They both look at each other, looking at me with a smile. "The surf shop is definitely hiring."

I raise a brow, "Thank you, I'll check there first."

She nods, "Chase works there and his co-worker just quit so I'm sure you'll get the job." She explains.

That sounds way too simple but I nod nonetheless. The two of them are lifeguards at the kids center so they leave. I make my way to the store that has a giant blue surfboard at the entrance.

Chase stands at the register, his head lifting when the bell rings.

A smile takes over his face. "You're new." He jokes. "How may I help you?"

I put my hands on the counter, looking around. "Your sister mentioned there being an open position."

He nods, grabbing something from under the counter. He places a paper in front of me, the words application printed in bold letters at the top.

"She skims through it and calls you if you've got the job or not. Honestly, I'm positive you'll get it." He chuckles.

I take a pen from the cup on the counter, filling it out. It takes me a few minutes before I complete it. Handing it back to him and placing the pen back.

I open my mouth but quickly close it when the bell rings again. A girl with blonde hair walks in. She smiles when her eyes land on Chase.

She leans over the counter, her bright red acrylic nails scraping the surface. "Are you coming over later?" She asks completely ignoring me.

I stand back searching for his eyes. He gives me a small smile before clearing his throat.

"I can't, I have to help my parents with something." He tells her.

The blonde finally turns to me and scowls. "Why are you still here?" She says harshly.

I raise a brow but keep quiet. We stare at each other until Chase speaks up.

"Kayla, I'm working right now. I'll see you on Friday." He sighs.

She's fuming, her eyes narrowed as she glares at him. "You keep making excuses when just two months ago you were begging to be with me." She adds.

I really think I should go, this seems very private. I stand back to walk away discreetly but Chase stops me.

He gives me a brief look before setting his attention on her. "Two months ago I didn't know that you were hooking up with someone else."

She retaliates, "I never cheated on you!" Her nostrils flare and I can practically see the steam coming out of her ears. "I love you and we're figuring this out." She demands.

Chase studies my face before shrugging. "We can do whatever you want when I'm not busy."

Seeming satisfied with his answer Kayla nods. "Bye. I love you." She smiles triumphantly giving me a once over.

Chase doesn't respond only watching her leave. His eyes flash with a hint of annoyance before he shakes his head.

I bite my lip feeling extremely awkward. "Thank you for the application."

"No problem and I'm really sorry about that." He says sheepishly.

I tell him it's no big deal, the two of us feeling embarrassed. Although I hide mine to make him feel better about it.

"I should get going."

Chase smiles but quickly remembers something. "Actually, there's a party at the beach on Friday. If you'd like to come?" He asks with a hopeful smile.

I agree and let him know that I'll be there. With one last smile, I turn to leave and make it out the door. I must've been in there for longer than I expected.

Deciding to enjoy the weather and the fact that the beach is not yet crowded, I walk around. Holding my sandals in one hand and letting the fresh air hit me. The sand feels warm but not enough to burn.

I smile and allow myself to close my eyes. I never knew I needed to feel this type of peace until now.

Unfortunately, I have to leave because everyone decided to arrive. I have laundry to do anyway so it's fine.

Stopping on my way home, I grab some food to eat while I watch whatever I can find. Alice is all about shows and showing me the series she loves.

While I throw in my clothes in the washer, my phone rings from my bedroom. I let it ring until I'm done. Picking my phone up from my bed I see Thomas' name on the screen.

We have an appointment tomorrow for our first ultrasound. But I doubt it has anything to do with that.

I call him back, getting comfortable on the couch. "What's wrong?" I immediately ask.

"Nothing serious, I have a quick question though." I hear beeping and papers rustling, wondering why he's calling me at work.

I nod though he can't see me. "Okay."

"Before you say no, hear me out." More rustling and cabinets being open and closed. I hum to let him know I'm listening. "The company is having their annual party tomorrow and my parents can't make it. Do you mind joining me?"

I stay silent, I knew about the party already. I really want to say no but Thomas would say yes for me in a heartbeat.

I hesitate but exhale before asking. "What time do you want me to be there?"

I can hear him smiling. "Seven, we'll drive from my house because parking gets bad."

Again, I completely know what he's referring to. And while I'm aware that my parents will be there all I can think about is being there for Thomas.

I also have to buy a dress before tomorrow or borrow one from Alice. I don't realize how late of notice it is until I check the time.

It literally is last minute but I can always figure that out tomorrow. It's really no big deal.

I had a lot to do today and so little time. Thomas, unfortunately, had to miss my first ultrasound appointment which he's still apologizing for. I get it though, my dad wants tonight to be perfect so they have a lot to prepare for.

Luckily Alice got a day off just for me. She's excited and she even sent Thomas a message about how she gets to replace him. It was a joke and he handled it well by sending her a picture of him flipping her off.

After the appointment, we have to look for a dress. I was planning on just searching through Alice's closet and wearing one of hers. She was certain that I'd hate them all but I was stubborn and looked anyway.

She was right, they weren't formal and I'd be showing everything with the smallest movement. She was more than willing to skip a day of work and tag along.

I leave her in the waiting area while I get my first ultrasound. The entire time I'm anxious and excited.

"First baby?" She asks.

I nod, my breathing staggered as she spreads the gel on my belly. My eyes are on the screen not moving away from it. I bite my lip a little too hard without realizing it.

She explains to me what I'm looking at before I see it. I breathe out, tears pooling at my eyes. It doesn't look like much just yet but just seeing for myself makes it so real.

When we're done, I make my next appointment which Thomas will hopefully be able to attend. I plan on sending him pictures, his only request for today.

"Let me see!" Alice says impatiently, ready to see the sonogram. I hand them to her as we both get in her car.

She gasps with a giant smile. "Holy shit. You're actually growing a human." She says in disbelief.

I laugh, amused by her reaction. I send Thomas a picture, pretty much getting the same reaction.

We make it to the mall and visit the first store of many, I'm sure. My goal is to find a dress, grab some food, and get some rest before tonight.

I find myself being overwhelmed after the fifth store and still not being able to find something I like. Alice is being patient which I feel guilty for even dragging her around.

I have three I want to try on, Alice gave me a thumbs up as I make my way into the dressing room. As soon as I saw the navy blue one, I knew I wanted it. It's the definition of formal. It has a v-neck and cutouts on the back. I love the way it looks and feels.

I open the door to show Alice. Her eyes light up and I'm assuming that she's ready to leave.

"Is this it?" She asks.

I smile, twirling. "It definitely is," I confirm.

Changing back into my clothes, I take the dress to pay for it. Alice goes to the food court to grab us something to eat. I check two things off of my list of things I want to do today.

Next is taking a nap before being around so many people who only talk business.

And that's exactly what I do when we get home.

Alice made sure to wake me up with time to spare. I have an hour of a drive after all. I do my makeup first and let Alice do my hair. She curls it while I text Thomas.

"Are you not afraid of running into your parents?"

I suck in a breath because of course it's been on mind all day. "Yes, but they'll be too busy to really notice me," I say it more for myself.

She turns the curling iron off, brushing through my curls to make them loose.

I turn to look at her noticing her concern. "I'll be fine," I assure her.

She gives me a smile. "Go get dressed."

I look at the time, going to my room and slipping the dress on. I take a look at myself in the floor length mirror. I'm satisfied with how my appearance.

Slipping on some sandals and getting my purse, phone, and keys, I say goodbye to my best friend.

She's in her pajamas, a bowl of popcorn in her lap as she sits on the couch.

"Bye have fun and stay safe please." She waves.

I wish I could join her but I've already told Thomas that I'd go.

"Bye, I will!" I call out, shutting the door behind me.

I let Thomas know that I'm leaving already. I won't be there for another hour or so but I'll be unable to use my phone on the road.

Driving in a dress is so uncomfortable and I have to pull it up to be able to move properly.

The drive itself is bearable with the help of the radio. I try to distract my mind by singing along and telling myself that it won't be as bad as I think.

These events are uneventful and I hope that after tonight I won't ever have to attend one. My parents attend many parties and company events but this is the most important one.

It's welcomed to every single business person in the city. They all come together and even have auctions to raise money for a charity of their choice. They even talk to each other to decide if they want to work on any new projects.

Anyone can go with a valid pass which Thomas has because he works there. My sister her boyfriend will most likely attend. They go every year to support my dad. It's a big deal since it determines if the company grows in the future.

If you're uninterested in the whole world of business, such as me, then it means absolutely nothing.

I arrive at the Millsaps home, stepping out of my car gleefully. My legs are cramped from driving. I fix my dress, making my way to the front door.

Ringing the doorbell, I wait for Thomas to come to the door. I hear his footsteps nearing, smiling when he pulls the door open.

"Hey good looking." He says with a boyish smile.

I roll my eyes with a smile. "Let's go?" I nod towards his car.

We get going in my car because despite Thomas having a flashy car it has always made me feel a little claustrophobic.

The nerves start settling in when we near the venue. I'm not sure what to expect with my parents. Hoping that they don't even notice I'm there.

It'd make things a lot easier.

(8)

- -

Thomas circles the parking lot, attempting to find a spot. My palms become sweaty and my throat dry. I've been here multiple times, I know what to expect. But I haven't seen my parents in a week and I'm nervous to be in the same room as them.

When we finally find a parking space, Thomas and I make our way inside. More people arrive with us, a line forming at the entrance. We're good to go and follow everyone else in front of us.

The party hall is a huge part of the company. The tall ceilings make it appear even more spacious. And it's beautifully decorated each time. With creme colored tablecloths and a centerpiece adorning each table.

I recognize a few faces from previous parties. A lot of them are new though which is a good thing for business reasons.

Thomas pulls the chair out for me as we are seated near the middle. Because it's just us two, we got one of the smaller round tables.

My family isn't hard to miss, they sit in the same spot every year. Right by the stage along with the top investors.

There's soft music being played that is just barely loud enough amongst the chatter of people.

Thomas notices me looking at him. "Do you regret coming yet?"

I tilt my head with a grin. "Of course not," I answer sarcastically.

"Good." He laughs, knowing I'm only joking.

A waiter stops by to ask what we want to drink and to bring us some appetizers. Everyone turns their voice down to a hushed whisper. The main company owners, including my father, standing up on the stage to greet us.

After the usual introduction, they take a seat to let everyone get situated. The noise goes up once again.

Thomas socializes with the people at our table while I take the time to glance at my parents' table. I tense up when my eyes meet my sisters' boyfriends. He raises a brow, giving me a smile.

He doesn't say anything to anyone simply taking a sip of his drink. He must be taken aback that I came but doesn't show it.

The auction starts up and it's my favorite part. The money all goes to whatever charity they end up choosing and it's so refreshing to see. They all bid higher than the next, my parents participating as always.

It goes on and on until they have the highest bidder. I keep my attention on the front, occasionally glimpsing to make sure my parents can't see me. I notice that my sister is no longer sitting beside Landon. I look around, not finding her anywhere.

"Bea," Thomas says catching my attention.

I look at him, his eyes focused on something behind me. I turn around to see my sister talking to Mr. Jones, one of our neighbors. Her back is facing me but there's no way that she won't notice me. All she has to do is turn a little.

Thomas gives me a concerned look which I shrug off with a tight smile. If she does see me then so be it. I'll deal with that when it happens.

I still tense nervously, secretly hoping she doesn't turn around.

To my luck Landon walks over to her, leading her the opposite way from us. I breathe out a breath that I wasn't even aware I was holding. I'll have to thank him later for that. He seems to be my hero for tonight.

Our food arrives and I'm more than happy to dive in. However, my appetite is almost nonexistent due to being so worried over my sister seeing me. I have prepared for the worst but it doesn't mean that I'll be any less careful.

It's been a week since I made the decision to move out. My mom hasn't tried to convince me to change my mind. I was sure she wouldn't let me go that easily. Their image means everything to them.

To avoid dampening my mood I listen to Thomas talk about work.

After eating, we just sit and talk with each other. This is where most of the business talk occurs. I can already see my father discussing something with an investor. He's always looking for something new to work on.

My dad is proud of his company. He owns a big part of it which he has worked really hard for.

Thomas gets ready to stand up, leaning down a bit. "I'm interested in meeting one of the other assistants." He says, eyeing the table across from us.

I nod, "I'll be here." I assure him.

He goes to the table and I'm left alone. At this point, my boredom is hard to hide. Everyone is too busy to really notice. I lean my chin on my palm, tapping my fingers on the table.

After three cups of lemonade throughout the night, I feel like I'm gonna explode. I take a quick look at my parents' table before making my way to the bathrooms. It's in another hall, the door being right next to the stage.

I make my way in, checking my phone for the first time all night. I text Alice, pleading her to save me before I hide in here all night.

Putting my phone back in my purse, I set it on the counter. Once I'm done, I wash my hands and fix my hair. I respond to Alice a few times, wishing that I could be in a pair of sweatpants and lounging on the couch.

Thomas said we would leave soon because I still have to drive back. I'm not going complain about it because I knew what I agreed to. So I'll just wait until he's done before we leave.

With one last look in the mirror, I get ready to leave when the door opens right as I'm about to push it open.

I stand aside, letting them walk in. My eyes are set on the floor until I a small surprised gasp. Lifting my head up to meet my mothers' blue eyes.

My mouth falls open, a similar reaction on her face. She's definitely more shocked than I am. I knew she was here obviously.

She straightens up, her brows creasing. "Beatrice?"

$$(9)$$

"What are you doing here?" She asks.

I nervously look at the ground. "I came with Thomas," I say simply, my eyes darting to find any sort of resentment on her face.

She nods, her eyes skimming over my body almost as if checking for herself if I'm really pregnant. My stomach is still the same or I would have opted out of wearing a tight fitted dress.

Her lips are pressed in a tight line. "Your choice is final then?" She asks. "You're having the baby?"

I respond with a nod to prevent an argument. We can do this anywhere but here. I came for Thomas and I don't feel like discussing such a private thing when anyone could walk in.

She doesn't give me a disgusted look like I was expecting. Instead, she gives me the smallest hint of a smile. "I'm proud of you."

My breath gets stuck in my throat wondering if I heard her right. "You're what?" I ask in shock.

For the first time in my life, my mother has said the words that I have been wanting to hear.

Her eyes flash with a hint of sadness. "I will admit fully to trying to control your decisions. From my stance, having a child at a young age is the equivalent to ruining your future. But your father and I have both agreed that we handled it the wrong way." I've never seen my mother show an emotion that doesn't involve her being disappointed in me.

I'm still bewildered but I take in her words before smiling. "Thank you," I say, meaning it in every way.

She nods, "You're welcome to move back in if you have to."

There must be some catch to it.

"Thank you, I actually plan on staying with a friend for two or three months and then move on my own." Her gaze on me, soaking in every word.

My mother is a beautiful woman with blonde hair and blue eyes. She has wrinkles on her forehead that are barely noticeable. Overall for someone who works all the time, she keeps herself put together every day.

I can sense her guilt and I'm brought back to reality.

"That's good Beatrice." She says, "Your father would love to see you." She adds.

I nod, tucking a strand of hair behind my ear. "Okay."

This isn't the same women that slapped me and wanted me to undo my pregnancy. I feel my stomach twist at the memory. Why am I forgiving her so easily I ask myself.

She looks at me once more before turning to leave. "I'm sorry again."

I don't get to respond due to how quick she leaves. My heart thumps loudly as I take in what just happened. My phone vibrates in my purse pulling me out of my thoughts.

I gather myself and go back to Thomas. He gives me a concerned look when I sit down.

"What happened? I saw your mom come out just now."

He searches my face for something, I smile to reassure him. "Yeah, we talked but I'm okay." I nod.

He doesn't buy it his gaze settling on my mother. She's talking to one of her friends but I catch my sister staring at us. I tear my eyes away from her scowl.

Everything is pretty much coming to an end. Thomas says goodbye to my father and a few other people. I wait by the door, wanting to talk to my dad but not knowing how to approach him.

He's surrounded by people, so we leave and I'm left feeling a little sad.

We get into my car, the radio immediately playing when Thomas starts the car. I rub my arms due to the night being a little windy.

"Are you sure you don't want to stay with me?" Thomas asks, giving me a side glance.

I lean my head back tiredly but mutter a no. "I can drive back."

He doesn't argue but I can tell that he wants to. I would rather get cleaned up and change into a pair of my own clothes. Though I do appreciate his concern.

We arrive at his house, the streetlights illuminating the driveway. I step out to get into the drivers side.

Thomas stands at the door, leaning down to look at me. "Drive safe." He says.

"I will. Thank you for inviting me." I tell him honestly.

He nods, "Thank you for saying yes." He chuckles. "Text me when you get home."

I smile, putting on my seatbelt. Nodding at his request.

He stands back allowing me to back out of the driveway. I wave one last time before pulling onto the road.

I regret not bringing a change of clothes because this dress is starting to feel tight.

The drive is shorter this time due to there not being traffic. Everyone is at home most likely getting ready for bed. I sigh, smiling when I park at the apartment complex.

"Finally," I mutter, texting Alice that I'm here.

She meets me at the front door.

"How was it?" She questions, letting me in.

The first thing I do is take my shoes off. "Let me get out of this and I'll let you know." I laugh.

Getting the makeup off and tying my hair up feels ten times better. The icing on the cake is when I change into something that won't squeeze the life out of me.

I join Alice in the living room where she's eagerly waiting.

Clapping her hands together she urges me to speak. "Did your sister try to start anything?" Is her first question.

I laugh, wondering what type of images she has on what might have happened.

After I've told her about my mom apologizing, we both head to bed. I'm exhausted from the drive itself. My bed feels softer than usual which only makes me sleepier.

I woke up feeling like last night was a lie. Even after a shower and breakfast did it feel fake. It's hard to comprehend that after being told what to do I finally stood up for myself and now they see how unfair they were.

I was proud myself for getting away from that house. So many terrible memories of being out of place and mistreated verbally.

But seeing my mothers guilt and regret made me immediately feel bad. So I pushed every single time that she made me miserable aside and accepted her apology.

Just like that.

And then I wonder why I constantly get screwed over. Because of how easily I let people get me sympathy.

My phone vibrates on the bed as I fold my clothes. Taking a second to put it all away and not worry about it later.

My dads' name pops up on the screen, a new message from him. I stare at the screen, so many things coming to mind. I bite my lip in anticipation, sliding to unlock the screen and pressing on the message.

Meet me for lunch, I want to talk to you.

(10)

My dads' apology was a lot more straightforward than my mothers was. He admitted to being so in love with the idea of his two daughters going to a top university. I reminded him that this doesn't mean that I'm giving up the idea. I just want to figure things out first and then consider college.

Overall, we both had a conversation that didn't involve one of us getting angry. We both sat there for an hour and for once he didn't try to control my decisions.

To top it all off, him and my mother gave me a check of a thousand dollars. For the baby. The short note on the envelope said.

He specifically told me to open it when I got home. An hour away from them, knowing that I'd be reluctant to accept their gift.

Which I absolutely was, my jaw dropped to the floor. That's nothing to them, just a small present for the way they reacted. Their apologies and request to start over have really helped me. I feel relief and a huge weight lifted off of my shoulders. Having their support is all I have ever wanted.

It's a big step forward from where we were a few days ago. It's gonna take some time to get used to. My parents aren't all that comfortable with sharing their emotions with me. They have always talked to me in a formal way as if we're acquaintances and not family. So for them to suddenly change isn't likely.

Healing takes time, we're all going to have to accept the changes.

Alice and I head to the beach, where the party that Chase invited us to is. I tell her more about my afternoon and how she never expected my parents to speak to me in the first place.

She turns into the parking lot, circling a few times until we find a spot. "Holly is next?" She questions.

I laugh, "Doubt it." We make our way through the groups of people.

My sister is a whole different story. One that is confusing even to me. I can't remember a single time where Holly wasn't insulting me.

Music is already blaring through a speaker. There are a few tables set up with foods, snacks, drinks: both alcoholic and nonalcoholic. From what I've heard, a few guys rent out the beach once a summer.

It's packed, most of them hanging out by the drinks. We spot our friends, to my surprise Kayla is here too. Chase stands behind her with an arm lazily wrapped around her shoulders. I smile, receiving a cold glare from the blonde in his arms.

Chelsea wraps an arm around me. tugging me and Alice along with her. She must have begun drinking already, her laughter becoming lighthearted as she dances.

Her eyes land on me. "You're not dancing?" She pouts, her brown hair in light waves. When I shake my head, she turns to Alice instead.

Jesse waves with two fingers, one hand holding a red cup and the other wrapped around a redheads waist. Giving him a slight tilt of my head, I smile with an eye roll.

Becoming uncomfortable with the dancing, I excuse myself to grab something to drink. Having to push through the sweaty and drunk bodies. I'm grabbed a few times, strangers asking me to join them.

When I finally make it out in one piece, I breathe out in relief. Picking up a water bottle I end up wandering towards the empty side of the beach. The sky looks beautiful with the colors mixed in it.

I'm sat in silence just enjoying the calmness of the setting. Leaning back on my palms to get comfortable.

A shadow looms over me, a gasp leaving my lips. Turning to see Matt, I hold a hand over my chest.

"You scared me," I mutter hugging my knees to my chest.

He gives me a lopsided smirk, blue eyes glimmering. "Oops?" Sitting right beside me leaving space between us.

Breathing in the fresh air we sit in silence. Matt and I have shared no words before this, so it's impossible to think of what to talk about.

I pick at a loose thread on my denim shorts. Lifting my head up to give him a glance. "Why aren't you with everyone else?"

His eyes are set on the sand in front of him. With a shrug he replies. "Because you're here alone, and there are a bunch of hormonal drunk teens here."

I press my lips together realizing how far I had walked. If anyone were to have followed me, I would be too hidden to be heard.

Matt nods. "Exactly. Be careful next time."

I roll my eyes although knowing to be more alert. "Okay, dad." I joke.

His nose scrunches up. "Don't say that again." He fake shivers.

My lips turn up at the corners. Now I see why Alice is so attracted to him. He says what's on his mind, much like she does.

"So... Alice is great, huh?" I ask, taking in his reaction.

He manages to keep a blank stare. "What are you doing Bea?" Pretending to not know what he's referring to I give him a smile. "If you want me to confess my love for Alice, it's not happening."

I narrow my eyes at him. "You can't hide that you at least find her attractive."

"I admit that I like her, she knows that already. Doesn't mean anything is going to happen." He sighs.

Not wanting to pry I let it go. "We should head back," I suggest.

Standing up, Matt grips my hand and pulls me up forcefully. I groan, rubbing where he gripped.

"Jeez, you almost took my arm off." I frown.

Rolling his eyes he chuckles. "I box for fun, sorry about that."

We walk back to the party, teasing each other. It's almost like we've been friends forever. When in reality this is my first time having a conversation with him.

The only ones we see are Jesse and Chelsea. "Where's Alice?" I asked concerned.

They shrug, too drunk to even stand up straight. Matt squeezes my shoulder in comfort.

"I'll go look for her." He tells us.

I stand away from all the dancing and stumbling to avoid being trampled. Kayla seems to be having fun, her hands all over Chase. I tear my gaze away, checking my phone relieved to see that Alice went to the restroom.

Feeling like a fourth wheel with the three pairs around me is how my night goes.

(11)

I got the job easily, it felt a little too easy. Chase did warn me about that.

The manager, Linda called me and we scheduled to meet and train. Once again, it was way too simple. I get the responsibility of unpacking and organizing new inventory. Meanwhile, Chase works the cash register and helps with his knowledge on surfing.

We both work from eight in the morning until two. Getting a break for half an hour at noon. Currently, we're on our lunch break.

"What do you think?" Chase asks, across from me facing the store.

"It's bearable," I say with a smile.

He agrees with a nod. "It's not bad, I got this job in high school." He says. "It's actually how I met Kayla. Her dad owns this store, among three others across the state."

My eyes widen taking in the information. That must be why she stops whenever she pleases.

"She's quite the character," I say. Remembering how stubborn she was the last time, and the number of scowls sent my way.

He bites his lip, with raised brows. "That's an understatement."

Speaking of, the bell rings when a tall blonde walks in. Her eyes focus on Chase as she makes her way to the desk. Our break is pretty much over so we pick up our trash.

I trail behind him and let him talk to her. Organizing magazines on the shelves and letting the music from the radio distract me.

Kayla shares her thoughts on me being here pretty clear. "So now you're friends? You barely know her." She complains.

"I need to get back to work." I hear as I make my way past them.

She continues to whine some more, making Chase sigh in distress. "Whatever, I'll call you later." She leans forward to kiss his cheek.

I keep my eyes on the box I carry. Stopping when my path is blocked.

"You don't greet your customers, that's rude don't you think?" She's mocking me, I can tell by the glint in her eyes.

I set the box on the floor, giving her an obviously fake smile. "Hi, ma'am did you find everything okay?" I ask politely.

After all, if her dad owns this, I'm sure she'd do anything to get him to fire me.

Kayla doesn't say anything instead looking past me to catch Chases' reaction. My back is turned so I only see her grimace and watch her walk out the door.

"I'm really sorry about her." I hear behind me.

I wave him off with a small smile. "It's not like you're responsible for what she says."

He nods with a grim expression. "Yeah but everyone thinks I'm as awful as her for being linked to her."

Continuing to stock the shelves, I give him a brief look. "I guess it comes off as you being okay with her actions. I know you're not so it's fine."

We work quietly for the last two hours. I can tell that he's deep in thought while I pass the time by counting how many times the radio station plays each song.

Our shift is finally over which makes me feel relieved. I don't mind working in silence, it's just slightly awkward.

Chase talks to the next two people who cover the second shift. I walk out, tucking a strand of hair behind my ear. I make it halfway to the parking lot when my name is called.

Chase jogs towards me, standing right beside me. "You didn't even say bye." He scoffs.

I walk to my car. "You were busy."

"Sorry about today." He stuffs his hands in his pockets.

"Don't worry about it."

"I'll see you tomorrow?" He asks.

I nod. "See you tomorrow."

Giving me one last smile, he waves. "Bye!"

When I get to the apartment I'm surprised to see Chelsea and Kayla sitting in the living room. I'm reminded of today's events, trying to maintain a smile.

"There she is!" Alice grins.

I kick my shoes off before turning to fully face them. "Hey."

I can already see a pair of eyes boring into my face. I make small talk with Chelsea, telling them that I'll be back shortly.

I could hide in my room for the rest of the time they're here. Or I can painfully sit through being around Kayla and her serious glaring problem.

Once I've changed into comfortable clothes I make my way to the living room. A movie I don't recognize is on but none of them are really watching.

Chelsea's eyes light up. They're the exact same shade as Chases'. Forest green and they both maintain eye contact which has always intimidated me.

Despite being twins, the only things they share are the same eye and hair color. I've noticed that Chase is tanner which I assume is from spending time surfing. Chelsea is also not as tall, being a few inches shorter than my five six height.

They talk about usual girl things. I definitely feel left out when they discuss boys. The only one I've ever loved got me pregnant which I'm not ready to talk about so I stay quiet.

Except that Kayla includes me in every conversation, seeing my discomfort very clearly.

"Anyone special Bea?" She blinks, arching a perfect brow.

I stop fidgeting with the pillow on my lap, lifting my head to look at her. "Nope," I answer.

She tilts her head, Alice giving me a concerned look. "No? There isn't anyone you're interested in?" She presses.

"No, Kayla, I'm not interested in anyone."

She smiles smugly my reaction is exactly what she wanted. "Okay." She lifts her hands up.

I feel irritated because that wasn't the only time she pressed me for answers. Chelsea finally told her to stop sticking her nose in my bubble. I hid my laugh, giving her a thankful smile.

They finally leave and it feels like I can breathe again. Kayla is surely not always like this, it must drain her being that persistent.

Alice looks at me. "Remind me to never invite her again." She says seriously.

(12)

The Fourth of July is a huge deal to my family. It's almost like the last day that everyone can hang out before being busy with work and school.

Things have definitely changed this year so I decided to not go. My parents both invited me which surprised me. They're still adjusting to being involved in my life and vice versa.

My decision to stay alone in the apartment is due to my lovely sister. This is her opportunity to say something to me and embarrass me in front of our friends and family. To avoid causing a mess I'll just opt out of going altogether.

I sit at the counter with a cup of coffee in my hands. Alice runs around trying to get everything last minute before she drives to see her family.

Watching in amusement, I drink my coffee.

She comes back into the kitchen out of breath. "Are you sure you don't want to join us?" She asks.

"I'm fine Alice, I have leftover pizza."

Her eyes narrow. "At least go with Thomas then."

Shaking my head, I mess with the rim of the mug. "You guys go, I can handle a few hours on my own." I laugh.

I can tell she's hesitant, and knowing Alice she would cancel just to stay with me. She sighs, agreeing with me.

"Okay, fine. Call me and I'll drive back as fast as I can." She kisses the top of my head. "Don't eat the leftover pizza either, you're gonna get sick."

I wave, feeling like a child. "Bye!"

The door closes and I'm left alone. It's a little past twelve so I finish my coffee and wash the mug. Gathering clean clothes to shower.

I take my time, scrubbing myself and washing my hair. The room smells like my lavender scented body wash as I dry off.

I brush my teeth, fix my hair, and head into the living room. Scanning through the movie section I select one that looks decent.

It takes the beginning for me to lay on my side until I'm comfortable. I figure that a nap won't hurt and shut my eyes.

I'm awoken by the sound of knocking. It felt like a dream at first, until I processed that I was even asleep. Sitting up slowly, I rub my eyes. Making my way to the door.

My eyes light up in surprise at the sight of Chase. He wears a white T-shirt and skinny jeans. In his hands are a couple of bags.

"What are you doing here?" I ask, holding the door open to let him in.

After he has set the bags on the counter he turns to me with a smile. "Alice was worried about you being bored to death so she called Chelsea."

I roll my eyes knowing that she would do something like that. "I'm fine." I laugh. "Is Chelsea coming?" I ask.

Rummaging through the bags, his brows are furrowed until he finds what he was searching for. "She stayed with our grandma. My parents had a house to show so they had to leave early." He explains.

I keep eyeing the bags which he. notices. "What did you bring?" I question curiously.

After pulling out snacks and drinks for us, we decide to watch a movie. Chase chooses one that he's excited for me to watch because in his words it's amazing.

I can't help but smile every time he explains something to me. The movie is confusing and I feel bad but Chase has no problem with helping me understand. He's so engrossed in every second of the movie.

When it's over we sit on the floor and eat skittles. I hand him the yellow and orange ones, never eating those colors in any candy.

"I've never seen anyone do that." He laughs, watching me pick the two colors out.

I shrug. "I think I focus too much on the colors, the taste is pretty bad too."

I grin when his mouth drops open. I toss one his mouth, missing.

We take turns, asking each other a question for every one we make.

"What's your favorite season and why?" I ask.

Not even thinking twice he answers. "Spring, the weather is always nice and the air feels fresh."

He makes one in, not surprising because he's missed three. "What's a mistake you've made that actually made your life better?"

The question is a lot deeper than intended. I could answer honestly but I'd have to mention Thomas. "Deciding to move here," I say. "The result of my mistake anyways." I shrug.

His eyes search mine but I avoid his gaze. "I thought you moved here because Alice needed a roommate?" I remember her covering up for me when we first met them.

"Something like that." Definitely a lie.

Relieved that he let it slide, I turn to him. He's already looking at me as if trying to figure me out.

"You look down when you're lying."

My cheeks heat up. "How d-"

Chase gives me a look before tearing his eyes away from me. "Your nose also twitches when you're annoyed. I noticed the other day when Kayla was taunting you." He says.

Pressing my lips together, I question him. "What do I do when I'm happy?" I ask sarcastically.

His lips turn up at the corners. "Your eyes twinkle."

I push him slightly, standing up to throw away the trash. "You are very observant."

He joins me, tossing the bottles away. I learned a lot about him. One, that he's very outdoorsy and a people's person. Two, not to show any emotion because he notices even the smallest things.

"Thank you for not letting me bore to death."

With a boyish smile, he slips his shoes on. "Anytime." He chuckles. "I'll see you at work."

Standing at the door, I smile. "Bye Chase."

I text Alice and thank her for worrying about me. Feeling grateful for them for even caring. When my parents ask what I did, I answer with a short response.

My day didn't completely go to waste, I enjoyed it.

(13)

All it took was getting to know Chase before realizing how easy going he can be. For the past two weeks, our friendship has definitely blossomed. From the start, I knew that he was the type of person to make friends right away.

Not having to worry about there being an awkwardness between us has helped.

He seems to be stress-free, meaning that he and Kayla finally solved their complicated relationship. She doesn't stop by anymore, making work so much easier. I like that I can come in every morning and have someone to make it enjoyable.

We have a few minutes before our break. Chase helps Linda outside with some new inventory while I watch the register. The bell chimes, assuming it's them coming back I ignore it.

"Bea?" I hear, lifting my head in confusion to meet a familiar pair of brown eyes.

Standing up straight I muster up a smile. "What are you doing here Thomas?"

He's in khaki pants and a light blue button-up tucked into his pants, held up by a belt. Thomas has always dressed nice, his casual wear is hardly casual.

"I had a meeting. Came to see how you've been doing." He looks around the store.

We talk nearly every day but it's impossible to hang out with him. Unless I have an appointment, I don't really get to see him.

The clock behind me reads ten til noon. "I'm doing good." I nod.

Chase enters alone, Thomas turning slightly to let him by. Linda must have left already. I rush to help with the boxes, Thomas gripping my wrist gently.

"Bea," he warns.

I swallow, nodding. Thomas lifts them easily causing Chase to stare at us with a blank look.

"Thanks." He says, going to the back with Thomas following.

They come back, both acting awkward.

"Do you want to grab lunch?" I ask Thomas. Might as well since it's been a while.

His eyes light up. "I'd love to." He smiles. "Want to join?" He asks Chase, the two of us surprised.

He sadly says no, wanting to get some stuff done before eating. I give him a small wave and grab my phone.

We order our food and find a seat. Thomas is awfully quiet, constantly typing on his phone. He looks up briefly. "Is that Chase?"

"Yes," I answer simply.

His jaw clenches for a split second, making me feel like I imagined it.

"How was the meeting?" I decide to ask.

Finally putting his phone away, he takes a sip of his smoothie. I keep my eyes on him, wondering why he's really here.

"The meeting was great." His tone his serious.

The happy laughter of children and the busy shops around us enveloping the silence.

Thomas doesn't get upset easily, his mood changed too quickly for this to be nothing. I move the straw around in the cup waiting for him to open up.

I feel him move in his seat before clearing his throat. "I'm sorry." Before I can ask why he elaborates. "I ruined your lunch."

I grab his hand that taps on the table nervously. He does that or bounces his leg which always managed to make me feel his nerves.

"Quiet lunches are fine." I smile.

I pull my hand back, Thomas gripping it back in his. "I miss this." He says quietly, rubbing the wrist with his thumb.

A few months ago I'd feel the butterflies. My heart would do flips and my cheeks were burn bright red.

"Thomas.." I say, pulling my hand back with a frown.

His jaw clenches again, looking back to the store before turning to me. I can see what his mind is putting together.

I open my mouth but he beats me to it. "I'm sure he's in there waiting for you." He grumbles.

"We'll talk later," I promise. Making sure he understands that nothing has changed.

I get back to work my mood shifting back to good. Despite the awkward lunch with Thomas, Chase managed to make me forget about it. With his stories of when he was younger and even things that he and his friends have done.

I've realized that Jesse is the only one that I haven't really talked to. He's always wherever Chelsea is, never being more than a few inches away.

"Were Chelsea and Jesse ever a thing?" I ask, they made it clear that they aren't anything but friends now.

Chase sucks in a breath, placing his hands on the counter. "I probably shouldn't say anything." He mutters to himself. "He's always had a thing for her, they fell out for a bit when my sister came out two years ago. He was supportive but at first, I could tell it was difficult for him to comprehend."

I nod, definitely not expecting that. "The girl on her lock screen is that her-"

"Her girlfriend, Taylor. It's a long distance relationship but they're doing a pretty good job." He smiles.

I think back to when they were at the apartment. She didn't seem to be uncomfortable talking about boys. Although she never said anything about her love life. Maybe she's still not completely comfortable with talking about it.

Our shift ends shortly and we say our goodbyes to Chase. He stays for a bit to wait for Chelsea. She's a lifeguard for the kids' pool area.

I make my way to my car, seeing a bright pink sticky note on the windshield. My eyes narrow as I get closer, looking around to see if anyone here did it.

In neat writing, the words 'Don't mess with what isn't yours' are written on the note.

I crumple it up tossing it somewhere on the floor as I get in. It's either a prank or someone being childish.

Either way, I decide to ignore it and hope for it to be nothing. The only thing I can really do is nothing but ignore it. There's no name, no written threat but a bunch of silly words.

(14)

It's been a few days since the first note was left on my car. That wasn't the first, I found one every day after work. There are a total of six crumpled up neon pink notes on the floor of my car. Each day they get better and better, warning me to stay away.

My parents called me earlier which helped distract me from overthinking. My sister and her boyfriend of four years are engaged. They want to plan a party for her in a few weeks and I told them I'd be there.

Going back to the notes I tell myself that I'll at least get Alices' opinion on what to do. First, we need a few things and I agreed to stop by the grocery store. Making my way to the cereal aisle, I walk away from the shopping cart for a few seconds.

I turn too fast, a hard body pressing into mine. Instinctively putting a hand on my very small bump I gasp.

The tall boy who looks startled looks down at me. "I'm so sorry, I wasn't paying attention." He says sheepishly, a phone in his hand.

Catching my breath from being slammed into I smile. "It's okay," I say.

Leaving the store with more than enough food for Alice and I, I make my way to my car. My eyes immediately search the window already expecting a note. It's empty and I feel relieved that whoever it is hasn't been following me.

However, I notice a car parked at the very end underneath a tree. It's red and way too expensive reminding me of the type of cars that Thomas has always had his eyes on. The windows are too dark for me to see inside.

Feeling skeptical I get the bags in my car and drive away. The cat doesn't move and I sigh, annoyed at myself for being so paranoid.

Grabbing all the notes, I stuff them in my purse and call Alice to come down to help me. My eyes focus on the same bright red car slowly driving past the apartment complex. This isn't a coincidence I tell myself.

"Hey!" She calls out, walking down the stairs.

I grab as many bags as I can handle and let her grab the rest. We carry them all upstairs and immediately start putting them away. My phone rings causing me to jump for the third time today.

Alice notices, a worried look flashing over her eyes. "Are you Okay Bea? You've been really quiet and jumpy."

Contemplating telling her now or waiting, I tell her to wait. Taking the sticky notes from my bag and dropping them on the table. Despite her being confused she reads them one by one before looking up.

"When did this start?" She asks.

I bite my lip. "Last Thursday."

She curses silently, pacing. "Have you told anyone?"

I shake my head. "I figured it'd stop." Truthfully I thought it was Kayla but she hasn't been around and I doubt she knows what my car looks like.

It would only make sense for it to be her. No one around here knows me and the only person I could possibly be hanging out with that has a crazy ex is Chase.

Alice looks deep in thought, rereading the notes. "The writing is almost written very carefully to avoid being known." She mutters, her brows furrowed.

We leave the topic, for now, not wanting to jump to conclusions. Alice said she'd park at the parking lot when I go to work and wait around for this person to leave another one.

Thankfully it's Friday and I'm off from work for the weekend. Going about the rest of my day and pushing the whole thing to the back of my mind.

I'm awoken from my sleep with several messages, my phone vibrating every few seconds. Sitting up, I turn the lamp on and adjust my eyes to the light. It's barely three and I'm only assuming that this is important.

Seeing Thomas' name I nervously open the messages, hoping that he's okay. Instead, I'm floored at what I see.

Every single message is laced with an insult. Not believing that this is coming from Thomas, I call his phone. It goes straight to voicemail, another message coming in.

I ask who it is, I'm positive that it isn't really Thomas. They stop replying leaving me frustrated. This person is playing a sick game.

It takes two hours for me to fall back asleep. My mind racing with thoughts and trying to put everything together. It's impossible and I decide that I'll talk to Thomas at a decent time of the day.

He often goes out to parties making me wonder if a girl possibly got his phone and thought it would be funny to randomly text me. That's reasonable enough minus the fact that this person is very aware of who I am.

After my shower to wake me up better I get ready for the day and grab my phone. There's already a message from Thomas asking for us to meet in an hour. I reply with a short response ready to end this mess.

I text Chase, knowing that he'd unknowingly make me feel better. We've gotten closer although I've accepted that I definitely like him, I've kept a safe distance. Assuming that he's asleep when I get no response I decide to make lunch.

Thomas has a long drive before I have to meet him, I have enough time to waste.

We agreed to meet at the beach, the parking lot surely being perfect for talking. Ignoring the bad feeling in my stomach, I park my car and walk towards Thomas.

I lift my head to see Thomas, accompanied by a smug looking Kayla, and a confused Chase. Having the feeling of something bad I glance from Chase to Kayla.

Thomas turns to Kayla, his arms crossed. "What the hell is this?" He asks.

Her eyes light up as she claps her hands. "Let's get this over with once and for all!"

(15)

We all watch her cautiously as she flicks her blonde hair over her tanned shoulder. To any outsiders looking at us, we look like four friends hanging out. Little do they know that she has caused all of us to be miserable.

"Alright." She starts, standing I'm front of me. "I met Thomas when I went to visit my aunt. We talked, exchanged numbers and went out a few times. I never realized that you two had anything to do with each other until you texted him and your picture popped up." Her smirk causes chills up my spine. "It was perfect because Thomas here is still in love with you. I took the opportunity to use him to get Chase back."

My eyes drift to Chase watching his reaction. His hands are in his pockets, eyes downcast. I then look to Thomas who is already watching me with his jaw clenched.

"The day I came here, she told me to see for myself." He tells me, giving Chase a once over.

My eyes are narrowed as I look at Kayla. "The notes were you?"

She grins proudly. "All me, I'm surprised you didn't tell Chase." She raises a brow as if impressed.

I scoff in disgust. "You did all of this because of jealousy?"

Kaylas' eyes flash with a hint of anger. "He loved me before you showed up. You ruined everything when you moved here."

"Your relationship was pretty ruined already."

Chase finally moves from his spot, putting an arm in front of Kayla to prevent her from coming near me. It shocks all even if it's a quick maneuver.

Her eyes are dark as she realizes that he defended me. "Right, if you weren't pregnant I wouldn't hold back." She says matter of factly.

The air is thick, my eyes focused on only Chase. His mouth drops open and then closes. He glares at Thomas everything making sense. When his usual bright green eyes land on mine I feel myself freeze.

"You're pregnant?" He asks, his tone is unfamiliar. Laced with anger, something I've never heard in his voice. When I don't respond he laughs. "That's just perfect.." He mutters.

Holding my tears, I swallow the lump in my throat. "Chase.."

He shakes his head, taking a step back. "You two figure this out." He points to Thomas and me.

I watch him leave with tears filling my eyes. Feeling ashamed and humiliated by all of this.

Kayla turns to us with a smile. "I've done my job." Her shoes hit the pavement as she catches up to Chase.

Deciding that today is the worst day of my life, I turn to go to my car. Thomas wraps an arm around my waist, holding me against him. I struggle to move, pushing against his chest.

"Bea, I'm sorry." His voice is a whisper, his chin resting on my head.

I find the strength to shove him away, not looking back. When I'm in my car the tears are no longer manageable. I sob, feeling weak for even caring about his stupid reaction.

Kayla got exactly what she wanted. For Chase to hate me, she should be satisfied by now. I'm more upset at the thought of losing a friend, being well aware that the two of has had a lot to deal with before even dating other people.

I knew I had to tell him about the pregnancy eventually. I was living in a dream world where none of that mattered. I didn't worry about what would happen afterward, only telling myself that nothing was going to happen anyways.

He was upset and that was enough to make my heart shatter. Was he mad at me for not telling him or for leading us both on?

Once I've cleared my mind and I'm all out of tears, I drive back. Alice tells me to drive safely which I assume that Thomas told her the minor details.

She's ready with a sad smile and my favorite cupcake in her hand. I hug her tightly.

Her hand rubs my back soothingly. "I can't bake so I ran to the bakery." She says through a frown.

Laughing sadly I take the cupcake. "Thank you."

We sit on the couch and watch a show on TLC. Thomas has sent me several apologies and worried messages. I would delete his number or even block it but that wouldn't be fair.

What he did wasn't even out of spite but because he felt that it was his only choice. I'm only frustrated at him for allowing Kayla to use him for her own gain. Although maybe he deserved it after how he used me.

I roll my eyes, I would never actually see it that way. I let things work out on their own.

Once dinner time rolls around and I've moved from my spot a total of three times, I stand up. My legs are cramped and my stomach growls in hunger.

"Let's make pizza!" I say.

Alice stares at me as if I just grew another head. Her eyes search my face before she nods slowly.

I laugh, skipping to the kitchen happily. Getting out the ingredients and searching for an easy recipe online. Between the two of us, we're not the best at cooking. Alice can make a few things, while I struggle to even make eggs.

It's embarrassing but I've learned that some of us aren't as good at things that others are great at.

The kitchen smells great as we wait for it to be finished.

"Do you think he sees me differently?" I ask.

Alice chews on her lip before replying. "I think it's hard to fully grasp. He must be torn, he definitely likes you or he wouldn't have freaked out."

"I mean we're friends so I'm sure that's why." Lie.

She rolls her eyes. "We all know you two would be dating if it weren't for the drama."

My cheeks heat up because she's right. Even if I had told him sooner I don't think much would have changed. It's still extremely difficult for a nineteen year to want to date a soon to be mom.

I sigh in defeat understanding that I'll have to accept things. I can't be mad at anyone. Maybe a little at Thomas and I for being careless, to begin with. And of course at Kayla for being obsessed and wanting to ruin my life.

Anyways, whatever happens, is out of my control. One thing for sure is that I need to talk to Chase.

(16)

It was silly of me to think that I could come to work on Monday and everything would be fine. Chase didn't show up and it got worse when he ignored my texts. I gave him space, deciding to wait and see if he shows up today.

He didn't, and I tried to justify his reasoning. Telling myself that it had nothing to do with what happened on Friday.

Linda helped with the cash register Because I can't work two positions. It's a lot different after getting used to being around Chase. She was quiet and worked with only the radio on.

It didn't feel right.

I hear her in the front talking to someone who just walked in. I continue to flatten out the cardboard box to make space. Linda calls my name so I go to the main room.

Chelsea stands in front of me a few feet away. Her usual smile is hidden by a serious expression. "Can we talk?" She asks, glancing to Linda who nods.

I follow her outside warily. "What's wrong?" I ask.

Chelsea is shorter than me, but I find her intimidating. Seeing her and her brother upset is another level of scary.

Her arms are crossed, her lips pressed in a tight line. "My brother came home distraught, he didn't say much but locked himself in his room. Kayla told me enough." She gives me a once over.

I gape at her, wondering what she could have possibly told her. "What did Kayla say happened?"

Her eyes narrow. "Why so you can lie about what really happened? You're pregnant with another guy while giving Chase false hopes."

I chew on my lip. "I need to talk to him," I say.

Her face softens at the vulnerability in my voice. I can tell that she wants to say no but she gives in. "After work meet me in the parking lot, you can follow me home."

I nod with excitement. "Thank you so much." I smile.

She looks at me for a few seconds before nodding. "I'll see you in an hour." Chelsea walks away leaving me alone.

An hour felt like days before my shift finally ended. Linda is also preparing to leave as soon as the second shift people walk in. Once I've gathered my things I stop by her makeshift office.

It has a desk and a computer, a few folders on the desk and some pens in a cup.

"I'm leaving now," I say.

Linda gives me a wave. "Have a nice day, I'll see you tomorrow if Chase doesn't show up."

Who knows if this will make a difference. Maybe he'll show up to work after we talk.

Seeing Chelsea's car a few spots away is enough to make me feel nervous. What will I even say to him? Will he shut the door in my face or tell me to go away?

She shows me a thumbs up, signaling for me to follow her. Doing as instructed we drive for a few minutes. My mind is swarming with thoughts on how this might go.

She turns into a neighborhood, every house looking as neat as the next. We stop at one with two cars in the driveway. It's a two story, the yard freshly mowed and flowers decorating the porch.

Nervously I climb out of my car, trailing behind Chelsea.

"His room is upstairs on the right. Good luck." She says, giving me a genuine smile.

I do my best at staying calm. "Thank you," I say quietly, following her directions.

I take my time to get to his door. Not even paying attention to the interior of the house but wondering if I should turn back around and go home.

My hand is already on the door before I can decide to turn around. Knocking three times and waiting anxiously for it to open.

It takes a few seconds, the sound of rustling and then footsteps before the door is pulled open. My heart beats faster at the sight of him.

His hair is messy and eyes tired yet he still looks put together. Despite his face flashing with different emotions, he holds the door open for me.

I stare in shock but walk in to take in his room. There's a full sized bed in the middle, black nightstands on either side and matching dresser in front. He has a tv and a gaming system along with a rack of CDs and games.

It's clean and organized which doesn't surprise me. I look away from the posters on the wall to see his eyes already on me.

I cross my arms, feeling insecure under his stare. "I'm sorry," I say sincerely, maintaining eye contact.

Chase sits at the edge of his bed, patting the spot beside him. He leans forward, clasping his hands together. "I'm not mad at you Bea."

Hearing his voice tugs at my heartstrings.

Confused I turn to him. "I kept it from you." I remind him.

"You never had to tell me in the first place. We both kept our lives private." He keeps his eyes on the carpet. "But you never mentioned that you and Thomas were working through things."

Giving him a confused look I say, "We're not. Thomas and I only ever talk about the baby." It sounds worse out loud.

I can tell he still hasn't fully grasped that. A small grimace on his face. "Right." He coughs.

"Would it have changed anything if I told you sooner?" I question, needing to know his response.

I watch as he stands up, leaning against his dresser. "Then I would have known sooner." He shrugs.

Looking at him skeptically I ask. "You wouldn't have stayed away?"

He rolls his eyes his lips tugging at the corners. "I would have managed to fall for you some other way." He chuckles.

I missed him so much.

"How do we solve this?" I ask softly.

Holding his hand out he pulls me to my feet. I feel my heart rate increase at the little space between us.

"I really don't know." He mutters, his eyes falling to my lips.

I inhale his scent smiling. "I came here to make things easier." I laugh, "This wasn't what I had in mind."

Chase laughs softly his hand lifting to my hair. "You're so beautiful." He says, a goofy grin on his face.

I swallow, aware that we still need to make a decision. Yet I can't help but be drawn to him, along with the feeling of everything being perfect.

I wrap my arms around his neck, "Let's talk about this later." I suggest.

He nods, on board with my very irresponsible idea. I lean in pulling him down with me. Our lips finally meet and I savor every second of it greedily. Running my fingers through his hair as his hands explore my body.

His touch is gentle and it makes me want more. My entire body heats up when he pulls me closer. Kissing for a few seconds longer until my lungs beg for oxygen. Our lips barely touch as we catch our breath.

We come to the realization that this is it. Pulling away and getting into serious mode.

We basically decided to stay friends and not let whatever happened to get in between us.

I don't think he realizes how hard having a kid around is going to be. But Chase is set on waiting around until the two of us have healed from our previous relationships. And until I feel ready to let anyone in again.

Despite yearning for his affection, I will admit that I'm not ready. My body is adjusting to carrying another human and it's already started to wear me out. While I can't put my feelings on hold, I can accept that this is how things need to happen.

I went home a lot happier than I when I left this morning. I know better than to get too comfortable due to how much has happened everytime things feel calm.

I still have Kayla to worry about. She watched the destruction happen and is apparently going away to college in New York. That doesn't ease my mind at all, I'm sure she'll figure out a way to get to me mentally.

I'll deal with that later though. I can finally sleep at night and stop wondering if he hates me or not.

A smile appears on my face once again as I sit on my bed with my laptop. Alice and Matt were having a makeshift date in the living room with takeout. When I came home, I ran into Matt who told me very nicely to get the hell out.

I told him that I'd grab some stuff and be out of their way. Alice said it was fine if I stayed, glaring at me when I told her I was leaving. I caught on that she was nervous and didn't want to be completely alone so here I am.

Anyways, now I'm stuck in here. None of that matters when Chase and I are on face time.

"You can come over if you're bored." He says, laying on his back with the phone in front of his face.

Smiling softly I hold my chin up with my palm. "What would he even do?" I ask with a laugh.

Waggling his eyebrows he responds. "We'd eat cookies my grandma baked and watch the rest of Friends."

"Scandalous." I roll my eyes. "I'll take you up on that offer some other time. I need to shower."

He frowns, "It can wait." We stay on the call for another hour.

Matt knocks on the door, opening it when I give him the okay. He shuts it behind him, leaning against it.

Closing my laptop, I toss it beside me. "How may I help you?" I smile.

He has a serious look on his face but his eyes have a glint in them. "You're actually pregnant?" He asks.

I stand up, lifting my T-shirt up, being three months my bump is noticeable. My shirts hide it but it's there.

"Holy shit." He mutters, grinning. "Congrats."

I thank him, sitting at the edge of my bed. His eyes search my face for something before he stands up straight.

He turns to leave before giving me one more look. "Next time I'm on a date with Alice, I better not see you around." My eyes narrow as he steps out. "Nice talk Bea." He smirks.

If he weren't much taller than me and had the muscles of a clearly for person then I'd tackle him.

I finally shower and eat dinner while Alice tells me about how it went.

"We didn't kiss because he said it was weird with you here." She pouts. "And because he doesn't want us to call this a date."

I frown, "As in you're going on a real one?" I ask.

She shakes her head. "This was our version of a real date. He just thinks that we should kick you out next time because he was annoyed with your girly laughter."

I bite my lip annoyed. "I see." I tease. "I know when I'm unwelcomed."

She laughs, shaking her head." Matt's just messing, he likes working you up."

"I've noticed." I nod.

He's definitely a joy to have around.

I woke up excited to get to work knowing that Chase will be there today. I'm glad that we'll be back to our usual routine.

He meets me by the door, unlocking it. "Hey." He smiles.

"Hi," I say, flickering the lights on.

We get ready for the day, the atmosphere feeling so much better. Today's a busy day at the beach as the end of summer nears. All of my friends will be going back to college and I'll be stuck working all alone.

Chase will only work three days a week. Linda is already looking for someone to cover his shift since he can only come in after classes.

Despite us being occupied most of the time, we both maintain genuine smiles.

"Are you doing anything this weekend?" Chase and I grabbed some food from the restaurant next door.

I nod, wiping my mouth. "I have to help plan my sisters' engagement party. I'll be back Sunday afternoon."

I haven't seen her and I'm just hoping that she doesn't throw a fit. She's the last person I have to talk things over with. It isn't as easy as it seems. Holly is stubborn and loves to make a huge deal out of everything.

It's her day to shine, I'll just go for support.

Chase takes one of my fries with a grin. "I didn't know you had a sister."

I nod, "She's twenty-three and a pain."

"Unfortunately I know that pain."

"We can trade?" I ask, wishing that my sister was as supportive as his.

Chase thinks about it before tilting his head. "How bad is your sister?"

I smile innocently. "She's the sweetest actually, loves hugs and walks on the beach." If only.

He sticks his hand out. "Deal."

Laughing I shake his hand. I love his playful side, which is what makes him so easy to be around.

I didn't realize how much torture it is to be friends with someone you want so much more with.

(18)

- -

Since I agreed to help my mother prepare for Holly and Landon's' engagement party, I will be staying in my old room for the weekend. It's exactly the same, nothing touched except the bedsheets that smell freshly washed.

I brought a bag with a change of clothes and a few other things. My mom is already in the family room ready for me to help. Leaving my things on the bed, I make my way downstairs.

There are boxes of decorations on the floor. My mom sits on the couch, wearing a casual outfit of jeans and a v-neck shirt.

"Your grandparents are driving down here, I need to get the guest room ready." She tells me. "You can go ahead and unbox the decorations that go on the table."

I nod listening to what she says. She leaves to go upstairs leaving me to the rest. It doesn't take long for me to finish, standing back to make sure it's perfect.

I leave the balloons for tomorrow like my mom advised.

I decided to help my mom with the spare bedroom. My grandparents live nearly four hours away and they're actually coming. It still doesn't make sense to me that they don't just wait for the actual wedding.

I would understand a small family gathering but I guess my mom wanted to plan this. And because a party isn't enough, we're all having a giant family lunch on Sunday.

I help my mom put the new bedsheets on, the silence making every second seem longer.

"Will you and Thomas start looking for a place soon?" And suddenly I prefer silence.

I keep my head down, my hair covering my face. "We're just getting our own places," I tell her.

My eyes meet hers and I feel small again. She doesn't judge me instead nodding. "Have you talked about getting married at least?"

I bite the inside of my cheek, discreetly sighing. "Mom, we aren't getting back together." I leave out any other details.

My mom would have never let this go. A few weeks ago, she'd tell me to get together with Thomas. Afraid of what people will say when they find out that I'm not with him.

So to my surprise, she drops the conversation. "I'm going to start on din-ner." She smiles.

Everything feels so different and forced. I can tell that she's trying to stop being how she used to be. Very controlling and difficult.

I simply nod and walk behind her, shutting the door. I spend the rest of the time in my old room. I worked today and got off at two as usual. The drive was tiring due to the traffic being so bad and I am starting to really feel it.

A nap won't hurt anyone I think to myself.

My head pounds as I get up. My arm fell asleep and it feels like someone hit me with a baseball bat. Wincing, I sit up on the bed to check the time, my eyes widening when I see that it's almost eight. I must have slept through dinner which explains my hunger.

"Bea?" I rub my temples to ease the pain, hearing my mom knocking on the door.

She takes in my disheveled appearance and frowns. "Your grandparents want to see you." She says.

I nod, my throat dry and stomach begging for food. "I'll be there in a minute." I guess I still have a chance to eat.

I take the time to go to the bathroom and fix my hair. I don't have dark circles under my eyes but it feels like I slept through an entire year. Sleeping didn't help at all.

I hear familiar voices as I slowly walk down the stairs.

Several greetings are thrown at me. My dads' parents sit at the table with my aunt Rose and her husband. I smile, the only thing on my mind being food and the terrible headache I currently have.

Thankfully they all talk and catch up while I eat my weight in food. My family is very old-fashioned so it really didn't faze me that my grandfather scolded me for being pregnant. The table fell silent when my mother broke the news.

This is supposed to be Holly's spotlight. I don't have the energy to argue or defend myself.

"I'm going to bed," I call out, already halfway out of the dining room.

No one stops me which makes me sigh in relief. I just want to lay down and rest. I can't forget that I'll have to be around Thomas tomorrow.

His family was invited and of course, he wants to come. I'll need all the rest I can get before dealing with my sister and Thomas. And whoever else decides to tell me that I'm ruining my life.

Everyone is driving me mad with all the rushing around. I push the pancakes drenched in syrup around my plate. I managed to take a shower before everyone woke up so I'm ready for the day.

The party starts in two hours meaning that my sister will be here soon.

Like expected, Holly and Landon arrive early. I watch them greet everyone while I sit at the kitchen island. She walks right past me, telling my mom how much she loves the decorations.

Landon sits beside me, smiling at me. "How have you been?" He asks, giving me a side glance.

"Good," I reply, "You?"

His smile widens, eyes gleaming with happiness. "I'm doing good too. Missed having you around."

I nod, we had somewhat of a bond. Landon is attractive, with his strong jaw structure and light brown eyes. He's kind and includes everyone in whatever I going on. It still confuses me how he's been with my sister for four years.

I will admit that it's cute the way he looks at her.

"Congrats." We both say at the same time. I turn my head to look at him, laughing.

It feels good to laugh in this house. After feeling so out of place for years. We talk for a little bit before he's pulled away by my uncle.

The party has fully started, and for an hour I've been sitting in the same spot outside. My parents' friends, more family, and neighbors have all moved to the backyard.

I tap on the can of Pepsi I've been sipping. Leaning my head back on the swing. I'm pretty far from everyone else, enjoying the music and weather.

The bench swing shifts as someone sits beside me. I don't have to open my eyes to know who it is. The very familiar scent of Thomas' cologne welcoming me.

"You look peaceful." He says and I open my eyes to look at him.

I hate that we can't have a normal conversation anymore. Things have changed and I can't just keep on forgiving him. Not without letting him know that I won't always forgive and forget.

He notices my grim expression, nodding to himself. "I messed up again, I know."

"At least you're aware." I shrug.

Thomas and I were together for over a year and it felt perfect. We've both grown together and I'd love to see him set a great example for our baby.

He leans forward with a sigh. "I'm sorry for all the shit I've put you through Bea. I really do love you and I want the best for you. I'll do whatever it takes to make it all up to you." His eyes meet mine.

I needed this, I need to know that he's not taking advantage of the number of chances I've given him.

"You need to stop letting your emotions do the talking," I tell him. "You tend to do things that sound good in that moment and it ends up blowing up in your face."

"I know," he nods. "I'm working on that."

I smile and hold my pinky out. "Promise that you'll tell me when it's too much. I don't want to feel like I'm pressuring you into being there if you're not ready."

His attention is fully on me, a brow raised. "I'll be there the entire time, there's no way in hell that I'd back out. Not when you do all the hard work and I have to watch you struggle for seven more months."

My smile gets bigger at his words. "You're gonna be such a good dad," I say honestly.

It's a curse that I forgive people so easily. I'm bad at saying no and I fantasize too much about everything being perfect. But if there's anything that I've learned it's that some people do change.

I've seen it happen with my parents. It must take a lot of realization and for something to happen before they do finally wake up.

Thomas is clearly ready to become a father and he's gonna have to do a lot of breaking old habits. I can't change him or the past but I can be there and watch him mature on his own.

The party is definitely not as bad as I thought. My sister and I never even crossed paths and she didn't even glance my way.

I watch with a smile as she laughs at something my aunt said. Landon stares at her with that cheesy smile, and I find myself being happy for her.

I want that type of love. The kind where none of my flaws matter and I'm appreciated for who I am.

Only one person comes to mind, making my heart race.

(19)

All of my family drove back home after the party yesterday - minus my grandparents. They wanted to make their visit worth it and join us for our family lunch today.

Landon and Holly spent the night to make it easier on them. I somehow avoided crossing her path now to do it for another few hours.

I start getting ready for the day, making the bed and cleaning up. I'll be driving back when we come back from lunch. I'm not sure where my parents picked to eat yet.

I slip the oversized shirt that I slept in over my head. Making sure my door is locked as I stare at my reflection. A smile makes its way on my face at the sight of my baby bump.

I showed Thomas yesterday when we escaped for a second inside. He was in disbelief, dropping to his knees to inspect it.

Holy shit, he had muttered repeatedly.

I jump at the knocks on my door. Quickly throwing on a summer dress and pushing my shorts down my legs. I open the door to see my mom dressed already.

"Ready to go?" She asks.

I nod, taking a glimpse at the clock in the hallway. "Whose car are we going in?"

I doubt the seven of us will fit in their car.

She clicks her tongue. "You can come with us. Landon is driving your grandparents." She clarifies.

After I've fixed my hair and gotten my shoes on, I make my way outside. They're all ready to go, dressed in their best clothes.

I slip into the backseat of my parents' car. The drive is mainly filled with my mom and dad having small talk. I stare out the window, only talking when they directly ask me something.

We arrive shortly to a restaurant I haven't been to. The grand opening sign hangs over the name of the place. It's a modern building with a lot of natural lighting from the open windows. I like that we can see outside.

We enter the restaurant, all of them talking to each other. I stand beside Landon, thanking him since he held the door open for all of us. Holly waits inside for him, taking his hand in hers.

My dad had made reservations so we're led to a table away from the entrance. Like any other restaurant, there's music playing to lighten the atmosphere.

I sit beside my mother, and across from my grandfather. He's still bitter about my choice to forget about college - for now - I keep reminding him. It isn't final and I'm for certain going to attend. Somewhere in the future but I'll do it.

We order our food which is chaos due to my grandfather being indecisive. We all made our orders simple and he gave the waitress a hard time.

I give her a sympathetic smile feeling bad for her.

"Just pick something to eat grandpa." Holly pleads.

Once that mess is over with we're brought over our food. The entire time they talk about plans for the wedding. I'm okay with being ignored, also curious about when they plan on getting married.

Unfortunately, my whole plan to go unnoticed is quickly ruined. My grandmother brings attention to me.

"Dear, when are you and that young man getting married?"

The same question my own mom asked yesterday. I suppress a sigh being as polite as possible. "Never."

My short response makes her eyes widen. "You're having his child, I hope you don't plan on doing things the untraditional way." She practically scolds me.

Everyone is quiet, watching our interaction. "I do plan on getting married," I say. "Just not to Thomas," I add.

If that wasn't enough to make her eye twitch in anger, she narrows her eyes. Looking at my parents with a grimace.

"You two are okay with this?" She exclaims.

I keep my lips pressed together to avoid causing a scene. Landon looks uncomfortable, his gaze on anything but us.

Before my parents can respond, my sister surprises us all with her response.

"It's her life, no one has a say in how she decides to do things."

I stare wide-eyed wondering why the hell she just defended me. My father interrupts before his mother explodes in anger.

"Alright, let's not discuss this now." He warns my grandmother.

We make it back to my parents' house a satisfied sigh leaving my mouth. Despite my grandparents and I butting heads I stay around for their good-byes.

Landon helps bring down their bags to haul in their car. They hug Holly, wishing her the best and promising to call more often. I stand to the side, getting a simple nod and a tight-lipped grimace.

I don't even blame them, I'm not perfect and I'm making mistake after mistake. To them, because I only do what I feel is best for me.

We watch their car pull out of the driveway, waving one last time before heading inside. I plan on driving back now, needing to grab my bags first.

My parents and the now engaged couple stay in the living room while I go upstairs. I pick up my clothes and other necessities that I brought.

I'm in the middle of zipping up my duffle bag when I hear my sister behind me. I left the door open so she stands there, leaning against it.

I stand up straight, eyeing her suspiciously. "If you came to argue, I'm not in the mood."

She rolls her eyes, walking in further and examining my old bedroom.

Holly is an exact copy of my mother from her blue eyes, blonde hair, and fair skin. We both got our tall height from our father, both being around five six. My hair is a lot darker and I've always been a little envious.

She turns to face me, "I came to say hello."

"Okay."

Her eyes dart down to my belly barely hidden behind my dress. The pattern makes it difficult to make out my bump.

I watch her as she swallows. "You are definitely doing things backwards." She confirms with a nod.

I laugh sarcastically. "Thanks, I wasn't aware."

Her lip curls up into a smirk. "It's your life after all." She repeats her words from earlier.

I nod, "Thank you." I say. "For defending me."

Holly shrugs it off like it meant nothing. "Don't think too much of it, I didn't want it to ruin our lunch."

I can tell that she's saying that to make it seem like she would never purposely help me. I keep my smile hidden instead nodding.

"Okay," I answer crossing my arms.

She gives me a once over again. "How does it feel?" She gestures to my stomach.

I stare at her for a moment before answering. "It feels uncomfortable sometimes, like the morning sickness but it should stop soon according to Google. And I get out of breath easily." I finish with a shrug.

She takes in my words, her eyes flashing with a hint of curiosity. Landon stops at the door before she can say anything else.

"Babe, we need to get going." He tells her, giving me a brief look.

She nods, "Bea is leaving too, can you carry her bag?" She asks him.

He agrees but I protest. "It's not heavy, I got it."

And because Holly always gets her way I follow them to my car empty-handed. My parents stand at the porch, watching us get ready to leave.

I wave at them, saying bye to Landon as Holly stands beside me.

"I hope you're not expecting an apology."

I look at her. "Never."

She grins. "Good, because you're not getting one."

I roll my eyes at my ridiculous sister. "Bye Holly."

The drive back to the apartment is hectic with Sunday traffic. I had a long weekend and I'm ready to hang out with my friends for the rest of the day.

I haven't been able to talk to Chase that much, but I miss him. It's only been two days I know but I'm growing attached to him.

I knock on the door, carrying my bag and wanting to relax before I have to work tomorrow.

Alice opens it, beaming when she sees it's me. "I missed you!" She pulls me in for a hug.

I'm ushered inside, Matt taking my bag and Chelsea hugging me. The smell of something delicious distracts me but I greet Jesse with a hug as well. I catch a glimpse of Matt wrapping his arm around Alice.

I'll have to ask her about that later I note.

My favorite person is last, his green eyes locking with mine. My heart flutters when Chase wraps his arms around me. His scent and warmth intoxicating.

I want to say screw the whole waiting thing and kiss him. But I can't and unfortunately, he pulls away from the hug.

It's hard to understand what they're saying as they tell me what I've missed. I was gone for two days and I'm welcomed in such a great way.

I can't help but feel a little emotional at how amazing they are. I've never felt so loved as much as I do now.

My eyes meet Chases' only making my heart swell even more.

My life feels perfect right now.

(20)

- -

We've been meaning to hang out and actually plan something to do. With school starting up, everyone but Matt and I will be busy during the week.

Chelsea's girlfriend flew here to spend the weekend with her. It was perfect for all of us get together and go do something. I thought they'd both want to be away from everyone else but apparently, Taylor doesn't mind.

I have yet to meet her, just now arriving at the carnival. Alice was eager to spend time with Matt. They finally got together and I'm happy for her.

I told her to go ahead and I drove my own car. I pay for my entrance and walk to where my friends stand at.

I smile at the sight of a petite girl with black hair and pale skin. She's beautiful, her light brown eyes meeting mine. Her hand is tightly intertwined with Chelsea's'

"Hey," I say.

She immediately introduces herself, complimenting my outfit. After we've established that we shouldn't waste a second we begin to head towards the rides.

Jesse walks beside me, now a third-wheel. With Alice and Matt, and Chelsea and Taylor.

I smile up at him, "You can hang out with us." I tease, poking his side.

He narrows his eyes. "You two are worse then them combined."

I gasp, giving Chase a brief look. He only laughs, rolling his eyes at his friend. Luckily the two couples aren't all over each other the entire time.

We stop at different booths to admire the art. From photography to paintings to drawings. It's amazing to see how talented and creative others can be.

We even take a picture in the photo booth. The seven of squeeze together to fit in the small frame. Multiple pictures are printed, each of us getting to keep one.

"I want to go on that!" Chelsea says excitedly.

She tugs on my arm, dragging me to a ride that looks promising to make me sick. I shake my head, hiding behind Chase. My stomach is too sensitive for that.

Chase looks at his sister. "I don't think she should go on that Chelsea." He tells her.

She pouts but sighs, tugging Taylor to the line. Alice says something about staying with me while the rest of them go but I urge her to go. It's sweet that tries her best to make sure I'm never bored but I can deal with just watching.

Chase doesn't go on which is fine. He doesn't seem to be a fan of them anyways. We wander away, wanting to see some of the things we missed. Might as well since the line for the ride is long.

My arm occasionally brushes against Chases' making me feel a warm sensation inside.

Being around someone you strongly want to be with is almost painful. When it's the two of us at work, I can handle the proximity. And then I see him out of work and I just want to kiss him. I want to hold his hand, and do cheesy couples things.

This is coming from someone who hates showing affection in public.

He peers down at me, "You're being really quiet today." He states.

I shrug, hiding my red face from him. My mind is constantly telling me to ignore my feelings.

I can't.

Turning around so I'm facing him, I open my mouth before seeing a blonde behind him. My mouth clamps shut, my heart hammering against my ribcage. Please don't be her I beg, my shoulders dropping when I see her properly.

She spots us, her eyes gleaming mischievously at the sight of us. She makes her way towards Chase and I and as much as I want to run, I don't react fast enough.

Chase turns at the call of his name. "Kayla?" He asks, shock and confusion evident on his face.

She's supposed to be in New York. Far away from me, from him.

She has a smug look on her face. She practically feeds on our vulnerability.

"This is even better." She laughs, biting her lip.

She closes the distance between Chase and her. Placing a hand on his chest, her finger slides down his torso. His jaw clenched at her touch.

He gently grips her wrist as I stay frozen in the same spot. "We don't want anything to do with you." He tells her, his voice low and unlike anything that I have ever heard.

She doesn't react, observing our reactions with a satisfied smirk. "Come on Chase, we can have so much fun. You always loved when we spent time in the bedroom." She winks, making sure that I'm listening.

A look of disgust passes his face, his hand blindly searching for my hand. Taking his hand in mine causes my heart to flutter but I'm brought back to what's happening.

"Stay away from us." He says one last time, not giving her a second glance.

Once we're sure that she isn't near us we both relax. My eyes study his face for a sign of reassurance.

He lets go of my hand much to my disappointment. Chelsea jogs to us, all of them trailing behind.

Her eyes land on her brother. "What did she do?" She asks, searching my body to make sure I'm okay.

I give her a small smile, "She didn't do anything, don't worry." I tell her.

Alice stops beside me. "Are you okay?" I nod, still worried about Chase.

The mood is pretty much ruined and I want nothing more than to take away his anger. We walk behind our friends who have suggested we grab some food and sit to calm down.

"Chase," I say quietly.

He gives me a glance, looking somewhere behind me. I reach up to hold his chin in my hand, making him face me. His eyes are glazed over with something I can't pinpoint.

He doesn't say anything but maintains eye contact. "We can't let her get to us, it's exactly what she wants."

He nods, his throat bobbing as he swallows. His hand lifts to mine that's still gripping his face. I can feel him lean into my touch.

I'm aware of our friends watching us curiously. But it feels like it's just us two.

I do something confusing to us both.

Standing up to meet his height and giving him the smallest peck. My lips tingle, begging for more but I can't.

I pull away completely finding it difficult to breathe.

I grasp onto reality, closing my eyes for a split second. "I'm sorry," I mutter.

His eyes burn onto the side of my face. My body is on fire, nothing making sense.

We manage to collect ourselves and join our friends. They've already ordered our food and drinks, not questioning anything which saves me the embarrassment.

I quietly eat, sitting in between Jesse and Taylor. It was awkward for the first few minutes but they get over it quickly. I refuse to catch his eyes willing myself to not look up.

I blame my hormones for not keeping it together.

Lifting my head is a huge mistake when my eyes immediately meet with my favorite pair of green eyes.

Tearing my gaze away, I pretend that I'm listening to whatever Taylor is saying. She's telling a story on something she experienced a few days ago.

My mind is too clouded for me to think straight right now so I have no idea what she's saying.

I barely eat, pushing my food to Jesse who happily takes it.

"I'm gonna walk around for a bit," I announce.

They plan on going on a few more rides. We've finished eating but to prevent them from getting sick they're going to take a break.

I almost slip out of their view until I feel someone right beside me.

"Bea." Chase breathes out.

I press my nails into my palms, not knowing what to say. I continue walking repeatedly telling myself to keep my expression neutral.

Chase doesn't let me go that easily. "Let's talk for a second." He pleads.

I step aside silently agreeing.

We stare at each other the air thick with tension. I sigh, chewing on my lip.

His eyes drop to the ground. "Bea, I thought we were set on waiting." He exasperates.

My mind continues to battle with my heart.

No, I can't I repeat to myself.

"We are," I say, not convincing him at all.

He nods, stuffing his hands his pockets. "Because we can change that if that's what you want."

I want that so much, and I was willing to try but then we saw Kayla. I can't be selfish about this and I have to think about how it could affect our relationship in the long run.

I shake my head. "We should wait," I say more confidently.

"As much as I love kissing you, it contradicts your words." He teases, raising a brow.

My cheeks heat up, hitting his arm. "Okay, no more of that." I laugh.

Now I have to convince myself of that.

(21)

- -

The aroma of coffee and baked goods welcomes us as we step inside the cafe. Thomas stands in line to order for us while I find us a booth.

We had an appointment for my four months check up this morning. I took the day off, and Thomas got the okay from my dad to go in late. They've fixed their relationship and are back to where they started - kind of.

It's the beginning of September and summer has officially ended. We still have summer-like weather for a couple more weeks. It's just incredibly annoying to have to wear tight clothing.

My bump grew from one day to another and I don't fit into any of my clothes. I went out the other day to buy two pairs of maternity shorts and bigger shirts. But I didn't realize how much it was going to lower my self-esteem.

Especially around my friends, I find myself being self-conscious. But I'm also reminded that it's completely normal and I'm doing great.

Thomas comes back with an iced coffee for himself, and a raspberry tea for me. He also got us a freshly made chocolate chip cookie each.

"Thank you," I say.

He smiles back, breaking his cookie in half. I do the same, enjoying the music playing from the record player in the front.

I stir my tea with my straw, excited for today.

Thomas must have noticed how big my smile is. "Do you want me to come with?" He asks. "I can take the day off." He peers at me through his lashes.

I press my lips together, looking down briefly. "Chase is actually coming with me," I tell him.

He nods solemnly, before quickly hiding it. "I'm always here if you need me."

"Thanks," I say with a small smile.

We finish our drinks and toss our trash away. Chase is meeting me here since one of the apartments are close to the cafe. I've decided to at least find one that isn't an hour away from my parents or my friends.

I figured that meeting them halfway is better than having to drive over an hour each time.

Holding the door open for me, Thomas leads me to my car. I hold my stomach subconsciously, a smile covering his face.

"I love when you do that," he chuckles.

I look down, my brows knitted. "Is it weird?" I ask. "I keep doing it," I mumble with a frown.

We stop at my car, Thomas leaning against it. "It must be some type of protective thing, it's not weird Bea." He reassures me.

My heart rate instantly increases at the sight of Chase pulling in. Thomas leans away from my car, a blank expression on his face.

He's trying I tell myself.

I catch his gaze, "Thank you." I end with a smile.

He stares at me for a few seconds before nodding. "Let me know if you find a place you like."

I assure him that I will, watching him walk to his car. I wave at Chase with a bright smile, getting into my own car. I wait for Chase to pull out of the parking lot first because he knows more about it then I do.

I follow behind, hoping that I'm not picky and find a place today. It's a process to get approved and because most college students are still looking to rent I have to be quick.

It's no big deal if I don't find something I like.

We make it inside, the leasing agent was a couple of minutes late. She shows us the bedrooms and bathrooms, telling us the features this complex includes. This one has two rooms and two bathrooms which are the main things that I'm looking for.

It has the room for me and the baby, but I can't see myself living here.

We go to the next one, and I fall in love with the area. "I really hope this is it." I murmur.

Chase gives me an encouraging smile before we are led inside. I tried not to get too excited but just seeing each room for myself made me positive this was it. It doesn't feel cramped and there's a lot of natural lighting.

The kitchen is open instead of in a corner like the previous one and overall I can definitely see myself living here.

My smile gets even bigger up until Chase asks the rent price. I nervously bite my lip waiting for it.

The leasing agent checks her clipboard. "This space is available with the monthly rent of thirteen hundred."

My shoulders slump, turning to look at what Chase thinks. His eyes are wide in bewilderment. To pay that much rent a month would mean having to be on a tight budget. I'm sure I can do it for the first few months but as soon as the baby is born, I won't have the funds to support us. Not without having to work which I don't plan on doing for the first three months.

Chase sits on the passenger side. "Living in the city is expensive."

I don't respond, leaning my head against the window. We went to four apartments and even if they are exactly what I'm looking for, the price isn't in my budget.

I almost feel desperate enough to accept my parents offer on paying the rent for me. It wouldn't feel right though, I want to know that I can do it on my own.

My eyes become blurry with tears due to frustration. I sniffle which alarms Chase. His hand immediately takes mine, rubbing his thumb soothingly on my wrist.

The amount of times that I've cried during my pregnancy is immense. I thought that people in movies were making it more dramatic than it really is.

I laugh, wiping at my eyes. "I can't even control my emotions." I stammer.

Chase readjusts his position so that he's facing me and begins to rub my back soothingly. He's amused, I can see it by his grin.

"You're adorable." He chuckles.

I bite my lip, leaning my head back again. "I don't feel it," I admit.

His brow is raised but he doesn't say anything. I feel like a completely different person with how much of a wreck I have been recently.

With a sudden rush, I sit up and beam at him. "Okay, let's go see the last two places. I'll figure out the rest from there."

"That's what I like to hear." He grins.

I watch him climb out of my car and get into his. I follow behind him, feeling extremely lucky that he came. Chase doesn't work today but he does have a class in two hours so we have to do this now.

I go in open-minded and remind myself that it isn't the end of the world if I don't like any of them. No one is rushing me to move out, in fact, Alice has been begging me to stay.

I don't want to bother her with a newborn and I would like to have room to put their things in. So in the end, I kind of need my own place.

We stop by my apartment afterward before Chase has to go to class.

I'm not disappointed about not finding an apartment, I'll just keep an eye out. Lounging on the couch with Chase is better than being out in the heat anyway.

I've been stressing myself out way too much lately.

Sadly we make it halfway through a movie before he leaves. I'm left alone again, contemplating going to work but decided against it.

Sleeping sounds more appealing to me right now.

(22)

Work is a lot more exhausting when you're pregnant. It's almost humorous if you're not the one taking five minutes to stand up after kneeling to stock shelves.

I sigh, lifting the empty box and carrying it to the back room. Chase eyes me when I enter the room again.

"Bea just let me help you." He exasperates.

I narrow my eyes at him. "I'm fine. We have a deal, you carry the stuff in and I do the rest." I say with a tight smile.

I'm done for the day, physically and in every other way.

"Are you doing anything today?" I ask, leaning against the counter.

He keeps my gaze, "Nope."

I smile causing him to raise his eyebrow. "Do you maybe want to get ice cream with me?" I ask.

The weather is slowly shifting to actually feel like fall. Not enough for it to be more than a little cooler outside. Plus I've been craving Oreos and creme ice cream all week.

Chase pretends to think about it before agreeing. "I'm always down for ice cream."

"I'll remember that."

As soon as our shift is done, we head to the ice cream shop in separate cars. I'm more than excited at finally getting one of my cravings.

I'm practically in heaven when I walk inside. I order with a smile, feeling like a little kid. Chase orders a plain vanilla ice cream which I tease him for.

We sit outside underneath an umbrella at a round table.

I offer him some of mine which he denies. "Do you seriously not like flavors?" I ask.

He chuckles with a shrug. "I occasionally get the mint kind."

"You're a grandpa," I say, laughing.

He stuffs a spoonful of ice cream in his mouth instead of responding.

We finish our ice creams but I know I won't see him tomorrow because he has two classes. And part of me doesn't want to leave yet.

"Can we go to the park?" I plead.

Chase nods, "I was gonna suggest going somewhere but the park sounds nice."

We walked the trail at the park while we waited for Jesse to join us. Chelsea had a facetime date with Taylor and the other two are currently busy with work and school.

We sit at one of the tables, Jesse telling us how much he wants to drop out.

His gaze drops on me briefly.

"What?"

Shaking his head, he waves me off. There's something he wants to say.

Chase is oblivious to his glances towards me. "This year has been interesting." He laughs in disbelief.

I agree with a hum. It sure has been.

"Who would've thought that you'd be single and that we'd meet this pretty girl." He points to me.

I laugh, rolling my eyes at him.

"You have a type Chase, crazy but stunning," Jesse adds.

I let out a choking noise, Chase laughing in amusement. We talk for a while more until it's time to go.

Jesse skateboards beside us to our car. "I forgot to mention that Kayla came this morning." His head is down, avoiding our eyes.

"Is she finally leaving?" Chase asks.

Jesse nods, lifting his head up to catch my gaze. "She wants to make sure you're not together."

I cross my arms, stopping at my car with a frown. "Why does she care so much?"

We drop the topic, deciding that she isn't important. Hopefully, she stays in New York and far away from. She constantly tries to stir things up only to leave and to give us relief before she shows up and does it all over again.

I got home an hour away to Alice sitting on the floor with a bunch of bags around her.

Gradually I make my way to her, "What's this?" I question, seeing baby items.

Her dark brown eyes are wide. "I bought a few things." She bites her lip.

"Alice..." I mutter.

She lifts her hands up, "I know we don't know the gender yet but we will soon, right?"

I answer her question with a nod eyeing the bags. I take a seat on the couch, letting her show me what she got.

We find out the pretty soon and I've decided to not find out immediately. Alice will be planning the reveal for my parents and our friends to find out. Thomas is okay with that, wanting his parents to be there too.

I feel overwhelmed because I still don't have my own apartment and I really want to get the nursery ready.

"This is cute," I comment, feeling the soft blanket. It's white, a gender-neutral color.

Not that the color matters to me, but most baby items are all solid pink or blue. It's hard to find something that doesn't directly have the words boy or girl on it.

After we've seen everything, I look at Alice. "So where do you plan on keeping this stuff?"

Her lips press together, her eyes darting around her apartment.

I laugh, standing up slowly and patting her head.

"I'll keep it in my bedroom!" She calls out.

I take a water bottle from the fridge, grabbing an apple from the fruit bowl.

Joining Alice back in the living room. She already has a show playing. I bring my laptop to the couch and begin my endless search for an apartment.

One that doesn't cost my entire savings for one month.

I wasn't in a rush to move out, but every day I feel the need to have a room for the baby ready.

Especially once we find out the gender, there's no way that I can contain myself from buying things. I have to keep myself from becoming frustrated all over again.

I shut my laptop, averting my eyes to the TV. Alice has passed out, college and work both draining her.

I turn the volume down and pull a blanket over her. My closet is empty since I don't have many clothes in there. It takes me longer than I thought to put everything she bought in my closet.

With an audible sigh, I get comfortable on the bed. My hand cradles my stomach, feeling movement with a smile on my face.

(23)

Chelsea volunteered to keep me out until it's time to drive to Alice's parents home for the gender reveal. They gave her permission since they won't be back for another week.

It's been hard for Alice to keep it to herself for the past week. She had to plan everything and wanted to make it perfect. I have to give her credit though, she's not giving in.

In a few hours, she won't have to.

My chest bubbles with excitement. Not knowing has been holding me back from preparing and such. There's so much to do in four months that it's actually overwhelming.

I get into Chelsea's jeep, greeting her with a smile.

"First stop is breakfast because I'm starving." She says causing me to laugh.

I agree with her, not having eaten anything yet.

Just the smell of food alone makes me feel like I've gained weight. I used to be good with not eating too many unhealthy foods, I can't say that now.

I look from the menu to Chelsea. "What are you getting?" I wonder.

She gives the menu another look before smiling brightly. "I'm going with the french toast, bacon, and eggs."

I nod, indecisive and internally panicking when the woman comes to take our orders. I quickly decide on chocolate chip pancakes and bacon.

"What do you think it is?" Chelsea randomly asks, leaning her chin on her hands.

I reply with a small shrug. "I really don't know," I say truthfully.

She nods, our food arriving. "Is it weird to be around my brother?" She asks, taking a bite of her toast.

I laugh, "Yes and no. I have this slight fear that he wants nothing to do with me because I'm having a kid with someone else. He never looks at me any differently though." I admit.

She keeps her eyes on me. "I can't give you any advice on that," She says with a snort. "But I know that he really cares about you."

We finish our breakfast and chat for a bit, going to location number two.

I look out the window to see where we are.

"A baby store?" I ask in confusion and a little bit of excitement.

She holds a folded piece of paper towards me. "This is from your parents."

I squint my eyes to read the neat little handwriting at the front. Just like the one where they gave me the one thousand dollars. Which I plan on using to buy whatever I need.

Pick out what you need for the nursery, we couldn't get you a gift and thought this would be better. Don't worry about the money. Love mom and dad.

I open my mouth in shock, I would have been perfectly fine with them not getting me a gift. It isn't necessary at all. I won't be having a baby shower not when they're paying for so much.

Chelsea and I enter the store and I'm instantly over the hesitation I had.

"This makes me want to have a baby." Chelsea coos as we pass by the baby clothes.

I give her a smile, trying to keep up with her. We make it to the furniture which is what is most important.

The prices are reasonable and I don't feel bad when I decide on a set that comes with a crib, dresser, and changing table. I also pick out a rocking chair for the room.

We spent a while in there and I'm ready to just get to where my friends are.

"Ready?" Chelsea asks with excitement.

I send a quick reply to Thomas, letting him know we're on our way.

"I'm so ready," I say.

The drive is filled with anticipation. My heart pounding as soon as we enter the neighborhood. We made it in time for everyone else to arrive.

Thomas is already waiting for me, greeting me with a quick hug.

Alice opens the door, a wide grin on her face. "Hello, welcome everyone and thank you for coming."

She lets us in, giving us each a piece of paper. It has the word boy written on one side, and girl on the other. I lift my eyes to take in the decorations.

The first thing that catches my eye is the banner hung up in the living room.

One side pink, the other blue like most of the things here. There's no hint at all and I have trouble guessing what I think the gender is. I go with a boy, putting it in the jar on the counter.

I turn around to find Chase but see my sister walk in. Her eyes find mine, making her way towards me.

"You came?" I ask in surprise.

She raises an eyebrow. "You weren't expecting me?"

I shrug, answering honestly. "I didn't think you'd want to be here."

Her face softens before she smiles. She goes with my parents who are already talking to Thomas parents. Two of his friends are here as well, talking amongst each other.

I go into the kitchen, finding Chase and Jesse there. I thought it would be awkward to invite Chase but he's so supportive and he didn't find it weird at all.

His eyes light up. "Hey, beautiful."

I smile, grabbing a cookie. Jesse stares somewhere behind me his gaze landing on me.

"Which one is your mom?" He questions.

I turn around to see my mom and sister talking. They do look really similar.

Chase chuckles, shaking his head at Jesse. "They're both taken." He tells him.

I nod in agreement. "Holly is the taller one," I add.

Matt joins us as Jesse mutters something about being single. I laugh, rolling my eyes. We talk for a bit longer until Alice ushers everyone outside.

She had set up tables in the backyard with food, drinks, and more snacks.

We eat and talk to each other until Alice announces that its time. She counts the papers first, most thinking that its a boy. I try to find something in her expression but she's good at keeping it neutral.

Thomas and I stand at the front, his arm wrapped around my shoulders. I don't think much of it other than him just being friendly.

We all listen to Alice explain how she decided to do it. She hands us a confetti cannon each as we prepare.

She tells everyone to count down, my heart thumping even louder.

This is it.

The countdown starts and my palms are sweaty. When they get to one Thomas and I twist the bottom.

All I see is pink, everything feeling like it's in slow motion. I gasp, taking it all in. Everyone cheers as Thomas gives me a hug.

I smile up at him. "We're having a girl," I say in disbelief.

His eyes are glazed over but he swallows hard with a nod.

We celebrate with our friends and family, feeling grateful to have them here. My reaction would have been the same regardless, it's knowing that makes me emotional. And now that I know it just makes it all so real.

In just four months I'll have a baby girl.

(24)

Standing at the doorway to the nursery, my heart swells with pride.

There's plastic covering the carpet and the walls are freshly painted. It's a start before I officially move into my first apartment.

A warm presence stands behind me, "We did well." Chase says, admiring the pastel pink walls.

I nod already mapping out where I'll be putting the furniture. It should arrive sometime this week which is why I wanted to go ahead and paint the room.

I lean my head back, Chase wrapping an arm around me. He smells so good that I find my eyes closing. We're both covered in paint but it doesn't matter to me.

"Tired?" He murmurs, his chin resting on my head.

I yawn, "Mhm."

This past week has been the most exhausting. From getting approved for the apartment to ordering furniture and still getting to work every single morning. Not to mention that my feet are sore constantly.

Chase leads me to the living room where we have a chair. I needed one to paint the top of the walls so Matt was kind enough to drop one of his off.

I sit on the floor instead before sprawling out on the floor. Getting up is going to be a pain.

He chuckles, doing the same. We lay there in the middle of my empty living room. I actually start dozing off, my back aching but not enough for me to move.

I don't know how long we're there for. My eyes snapping open at the loud voice entering.

"I brought food!" Chelsea exclaims.

I sit up, glaring at the oblivious brunette. She notices, sheepishly shrugging.

"Oops?"

Chase helps me up, his hand rubbing my back soothingly. He does it without even realizing it which I love.

He peers at his sister from where she stands in the kitchen. "You came alone?" He asks her.

I tune out their conversation still feeling groggy from being disturbed. I doubt that I slept for more than a mere five minutes anyway.

The smell of food wakes me up, my favorite fries being placed in front of me. We have to eat standing up but it's okay.

I feel a lot better after eating.

"Did you finish painting?" Chelsea questions, taking a long sip of her drink.

We both nod, happy to show her. She follows behind us, looking over my shoulder with a gasp.

It was previously white which saved us the time and money. I only plan on painting this room, liking the modern feel of the white walls in the rest of the apartment.

"It's so cute!" She squeals.

I smile, placing a hand on my stomach. I have some names in mind but I want to make sure that Thomas likes them too.

Speaking of, he's been really helpful. He, unfortunately, can't miss too much of work but he wants to put as much of the nursery together as possible.

I'm okay with that, I like that he wants to help.

I yawn again, leaning against the door tiredly. It's past seven, the sky turning dark due to it being mid-November. It feels like we barely have enough time now.

Chase turns the light off, gathering my keys and phone. Chelsea takes the trash and I make sure to lock the door as we make our way to our cars.

Chase drove me to the apartment to drop my car off before we drove here. I'm happy we did that because I'm barely able to keep my eyes open. I say bye to Chelsea and get into the car.

On the drive over my head is against the window, my eyes shut. The radio plays only further helping me fall asleep.

I'm shaken awake shortly, rubbing at my eyes.

"Thank you for helping me paint," I say, holding the door to the apartment open.

Chase gives me a smile. "Go get some rest."

I manage to get in bed after changing clothes and brushing my teeth. Feeling too tired to even take a shower although I'm going to regret that in the morning.

I've been busy all day, Thomas and I put all the furniture in the nursery. It's coming along nicely, with everything that Alice bought for her and what I've gotten as well.

I also have a couch now, and a tv stand. Everything has been ordered it's the delivery that I'm waiting for now.

I just feel the need to get her bedroom finished before focusing on any other part.

"Where do you want this?" Thomas points to the bookshelf.

I tap on the wall where I want it. "Let's try over here."

After hours of being here, we've finally done as much as we can. I admire it with a smile, glancing at Thomas. He wears a proud smile, sitting on the rocking chair.

It's comfortable and I'm sure that I will be spending plenty of time on it.

The furniture is white, the rug matching the chair, and hints of pink every here and there. I didn't want it to be completely covered in pink, choosing the very pale pink paint for the walls.

Thomas pulls my hand to stand in front of him. He's still sitting, my stomach inches from his face as he leans forward.

"You're ready to come out aren't you princess." He says quietly, rubbing my stomach in a soothing manner.

My stomach immediately moves, our little girl kicking against his hand. He chuckles breathlessly, continuing to talk to her. I simply watch, already knowing how loved she's going be.

It's also amazing to see how much Thomas has grown. He's more than ready to be in her life.

He peers at me through his lashes. "I have a name in mind Bea."

I nod, urging him to say it. I have a few that I've been keeping to myself.

"Madeline or Maddie for short?"

I scrunch my nose up, not knowing about that. "I'll think about it," I tell him.

I don't hate it.

He gets up from the chair, stretching his legs. "I have to get going, but I'll stop by tomorrow."

I nod, following him out to the living room. He grabs his keys, kissing my head. I watch as he leaves leaving me to clean up a bit.

To anyone else, we would look like a couple. Thomas has just been really friendly recently. Not in a flirty way either, I know his intentions aren't to stir anything up between Chase and me.

I appreciate both of them for not being immature about it. They've been in the same room a few times now and they actually greet each other.

It was surprising to me at first too.

After picking up the trash and sitting in the nursery just admiring it, I'm ready to meet with my friends. We're not doing anything other than hanging out at the apartment and eating most likely.

I lock the door and start walking towards my car. It's cold outside, my thin leggings being a bad idea to wear today. With a huff, I make it into my car. The heat immediately blasting when I turn the key.

They're already eating takeout when I make it there. I think I've eaten enough for a whole family of bears this entire pregnancy.

The tv is playing a horror movie because Jesse got to pick what we watched.

I curl up as best as I can, jumping constantly but nothing beats Chelsea shrills.

Matt and Alice are cuddled up on the floor, a blanket over them. I smile as his hand plays with her hair. He's such a softy when it comes to her.

Feeling a hand on mine, I look up at the most beautiful green eyes ever.

It's such an amazing feeling every time he does something as small as looks at me. I loved Thomas when we were together, but it never felt like this. Maybe because I met him when I was so young and I always had a crush on him. He was the only boy that I really grew to care about.

I swore we would be together forever.

Things didn't end right but I'm so proud of where we stand now. I wouldn't change how things are ever, no matter how complicated it gets.

I squeeze Chase's hand gently, my smile getting bigger.

This feels right.

I have made enough mistakes in my life to know this isn't one of them. But I'll make plenty of those to make up for it.

Looks like I'm not so perfect after all.

(25) Epilogue

Chase has been acting strange all day. He would constantly check the time and couldn't seem to sit still. I figured that he was stressed with work or something although he's normally good at handling it.

Thankfully it's Saturday and we have plans for tonight.

I'm in the middle of doing my hair, unplugging the curling iron. I smile at the feel of a firm chest behind me and hands at my waist.

"Baby, you're distracting me," I say, turning my head to give him a kiss.

His face buries in my neck, mumbling something about how good I look. I'm wearing athletic shorts and a tank top. Chase is always complimenting me every chance he gets.

Instead of attempting to do my makeup while he's kissing my neck, I turn around to fully face him. He looks exactly the same except for more mature.

One of his hands lifts to the back of my neck, kissing me sweetly. It quickly shifts into a heated kiss. Our hands exploring each other. I leave kisses at his jaw, trailing them down to his neck.

His low moan makes me want to have a quicky here. We've mastered those by now.

He seems to have the same idea. "We have an hour we ca-"

He's cut off by a loud squeal. "Daddy! We were playing Barbies." My three-year-old stomps into the bathroom, glaring at him.

Her light brown hair is in lopsided pigtails that Chase did this morning. She only likes when he does her hair because in her words he doesn't pull her hair out.

I'll try to redo them before we have to leave.

I bite my lip, giving him a glance before letting her drag him away. He's definitely frustrated right now because I am.

I finish getting ready, slipping on a dark red dress. Chase wanted to take Maddie and me to the beach, there's a fancy restaurant that opened up and he's been wanting to try it.

I asked him if he wanted Thomas to take her for a bit but he persists to have her there. I'm still here hesitant due to how picky she is.

I enter our bedroom, picking up one of Chases' jackets. I feel something heavy, feeling the pockets but my phone rings before I can check. It must be his keys or something.

I answer after seeing it's Alice. "Hey." I smile.

"Hey, have you left yet?" She sounds out of breath.

"No.." I answer. "Why?"

She laughs nervously. "Sorry, wrong number."

I pull the phone back to see that she hung up. Why is everyone acting so weird today?

I ignore it and go save Chase from Maddie before she tries to paint his nails again. They're in the playroom, building with blocks.

Chase lifts his head up, noticing me in the doorway. His eyes light up before he eyes my dress. I tell him to get ready, blushing when he discreetly brushes his hand on my waist.

"Mommy, what's a propose?" Maddie asks when I sit down to play with her.

I frown, shrugging. "I'm sorry baby, I'm not sure." She must have heard it on tv or something.

I eventually get her ready, being able to fix her hair. We walk into the living room, Chase waiting for us. He's wearing black dress pants with a button up tucked in.

He winks when he sees me staring. I roll my eyes with a grin. He gets us all out the door before we're late.

On the drive there I notice him becoming nervous again. All I can do is hold his hand, hoping this relaxes him. We listen to Maddie sing the entire soundtrack to a Disney movie.

Who wouldn't become less stressed at that.

"You're so beautiful." Chase whispers, I turn around after getting Maddie out of her car seat.

Even after four years of being together, his words still make me blush. That's how I know that I made the right choice to give us a try.

The restaurant is packed and filled with wealthy people. Chase made reservations a few days ago, after being on a waitlist. That's how bad it is.

We're seated in a corner and away from everyone else.

"What?" I ask, wondering why he keeps looking at me like that.

Chase shrugs. "Because love you." He says in an obvious tone.

"I love you too."

Maddie tugs at my arm, gesturing for me lean down. She whispers in my ear about how she wants chicken nuggets.

I laugh explaining to her that they don't have those here. Luckily she's past the whole throwing tantrums in public phase. She simply pouts and glares at the table. She understands that she can't always get what she wants.

We manage to order after waiting for fifteen minutes. The food arrived fairly quickly and Maddie actually ate most of hers.

We pay for our dinner and decide to walk around the beach. It was Chase's suggestion or plan since he already had mentioned it to me.

I hear someone behind us, turning at the familiar voice of my best friend. Alice grins as she nears us, immediately lifting Maddie up.

"Wow, what a surprise." She says.

I nod, although I don't know why she would casually be at the beach at night.

Chase takes my hand after greeting Alice. "Let's go for a walk."

Maddie shakes her head, clinging onto her favorite person besides Chase.

Alice waves us off. "You two go, I brought toys for us to play with." She pulls out two barbies from her bag.

I eye her suspiciously. "Do you normally bring toys to the beach at night?"

Her bottom lip is tugged between her teeth, giving Chase a brief look. "Yes?" She answers nervously.

I give her one last look and lead Chase away from them. Alice has been a big help since the second I told her I was pregnant. Never once has she left my side or asked for some sort of payment.

Three months ago, Matt and Alice broke up again. They've been off and on so I thought it was temporary until he left the next day. She's been a wreck but tries to hide it from everyone.

I hope they both figure things out. I hate seeing them so distraught.

The soothing sounds of the waves pull me out of my thoughts.

I wrap my arms around Chase, inhaling his scent. "Can you tell me why you're so tense?" I ask.

He visibly swallows staring so intensely at me that it makes my insides heat up.

I wait for his response, confused when he pulls back before kneeling in front of me. It's not until he pulls out a box from his pocket that I realize what's happening.

My heart thumps loudly in my ears. "What are you doing?" My voice comes out very soft almost in pleading way.

"Beatrice Callaway I love you. I've been wanting this for so long now but it never felt right. You're the best thing that has ever happened to me. I can't wait to have kids with you. And to spend the rest of my life loving you." His voice cracks making my breath hitch. "Will you marry me?"

I nod, although my vision is blurry. "Yes. I love you so much." I practically sob.

He slips the ring on, standing up to wipe my tears. I wrap my arms around his neck, kissing him softly.

I hear cute giggles coming from behind me. Turning around to see Alice wiping at her own eyes. Maddie runs to Chase, squealing happily.

"You knew!" I gasp, pointing at Alice.

She nods, giving me a hug. "I'm so happy for you."

I give my beautiful daughter and fiance a hug. I never would have thought that this would be my life. I love every bit of it, from my friends to my family.

My life feels perfect and almost unreal. I'm not complaining though.

The end!!

www.ingramcontent.com/pod-product-compliance
Lightning Source LLC
Chambersburg PA
CBHW070404200726
48294CB00003B/1087